SIR LADYBUG

and the
QUEEN BEE

Corey R. Tabor

BALZER + BRAY
Imprints of HarperCollins Publishers

Balzer + Bray is an imprint of HarperCollins Publishers.

HarperAlley is an imprint of HarperCollins Publishers.

Sir Ladybug and the Queen Bee

For information address HarperCollins Children's Books, a division of HarperCollins Publishers, 195 Broadway, New York, NY 10007.
www.harpercollinschildrens.com

ISBN 978-0-06-306909-1 (trade bdg.)

The art for this book was created digitally.
Typography by Dana Fritts and Corey R. Tabor
22 23 24 25 26 RTLO 10 9 8 7 6 5 4 3 2 1
❖
First Edition

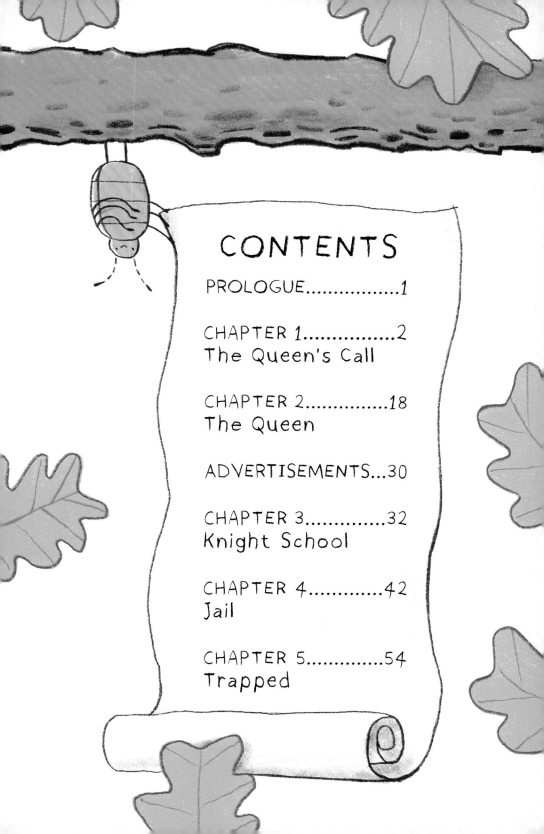

CONTENTS

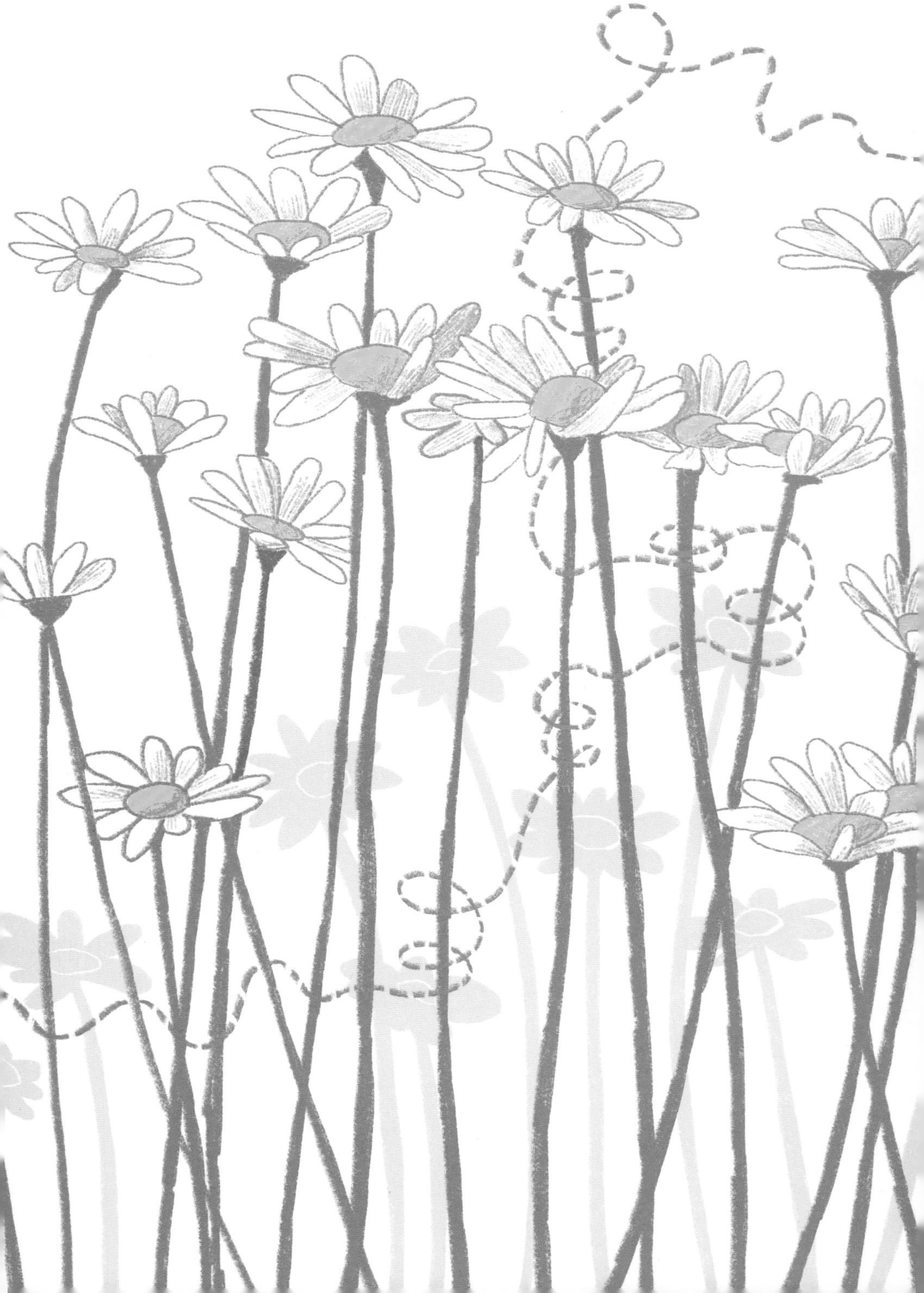

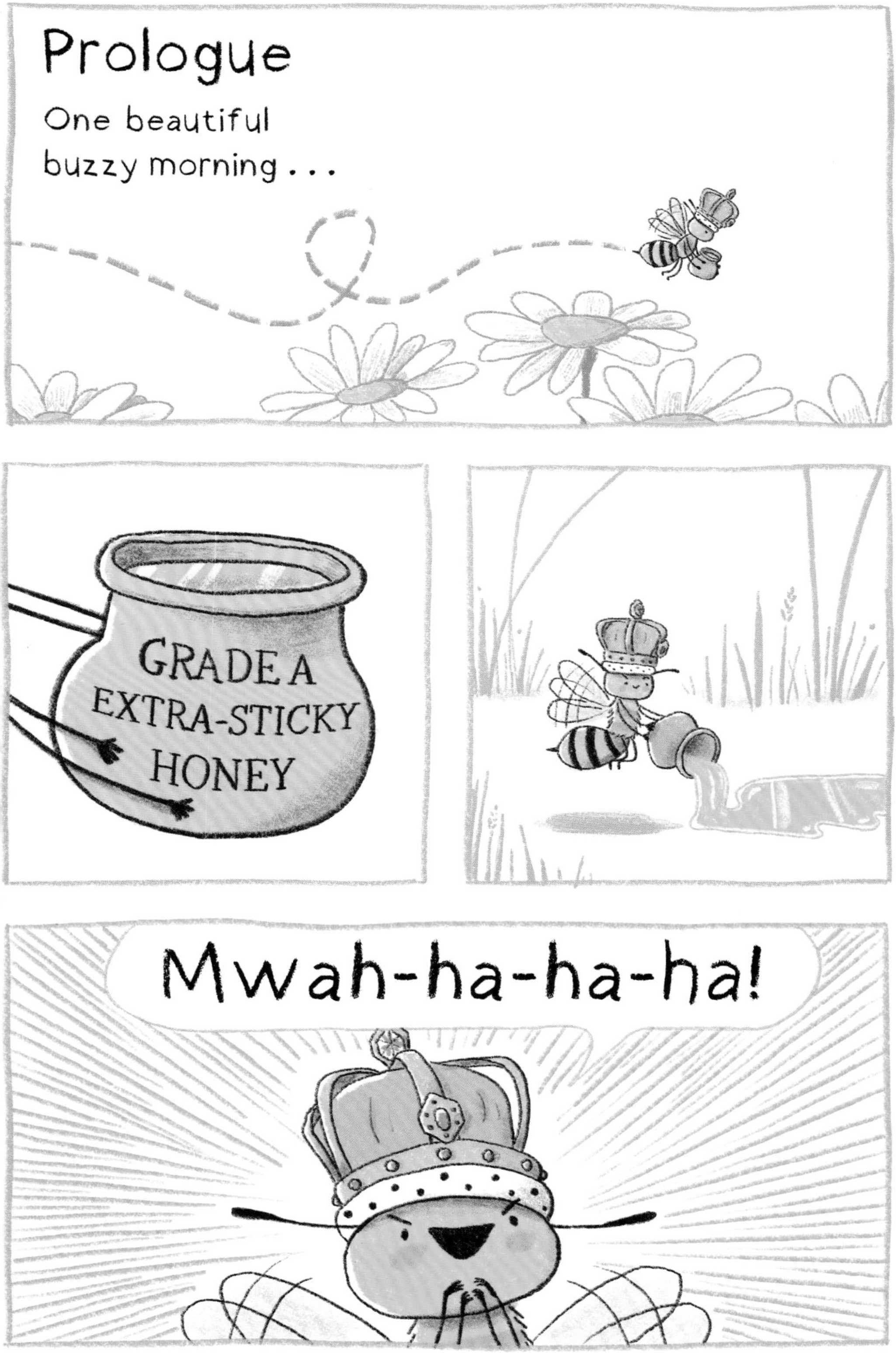
Prologue
One beautiful buzzy morning . . .
GRADE A EXTRA-STICKY HONEY
Mwah-ha-ha-ha!

Chapter 1: The Queen's Call

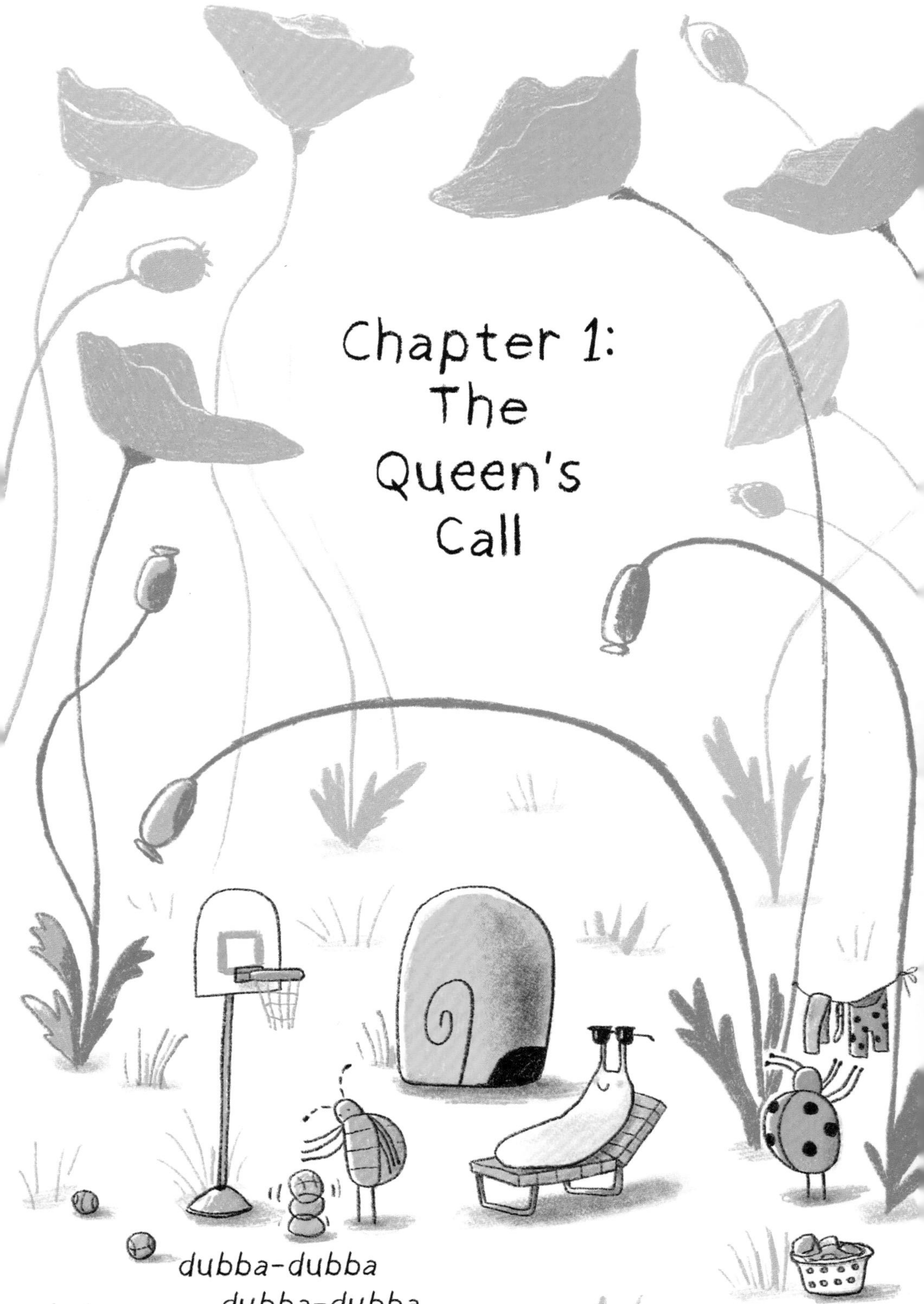
dubba-dubba
dubba-dubba

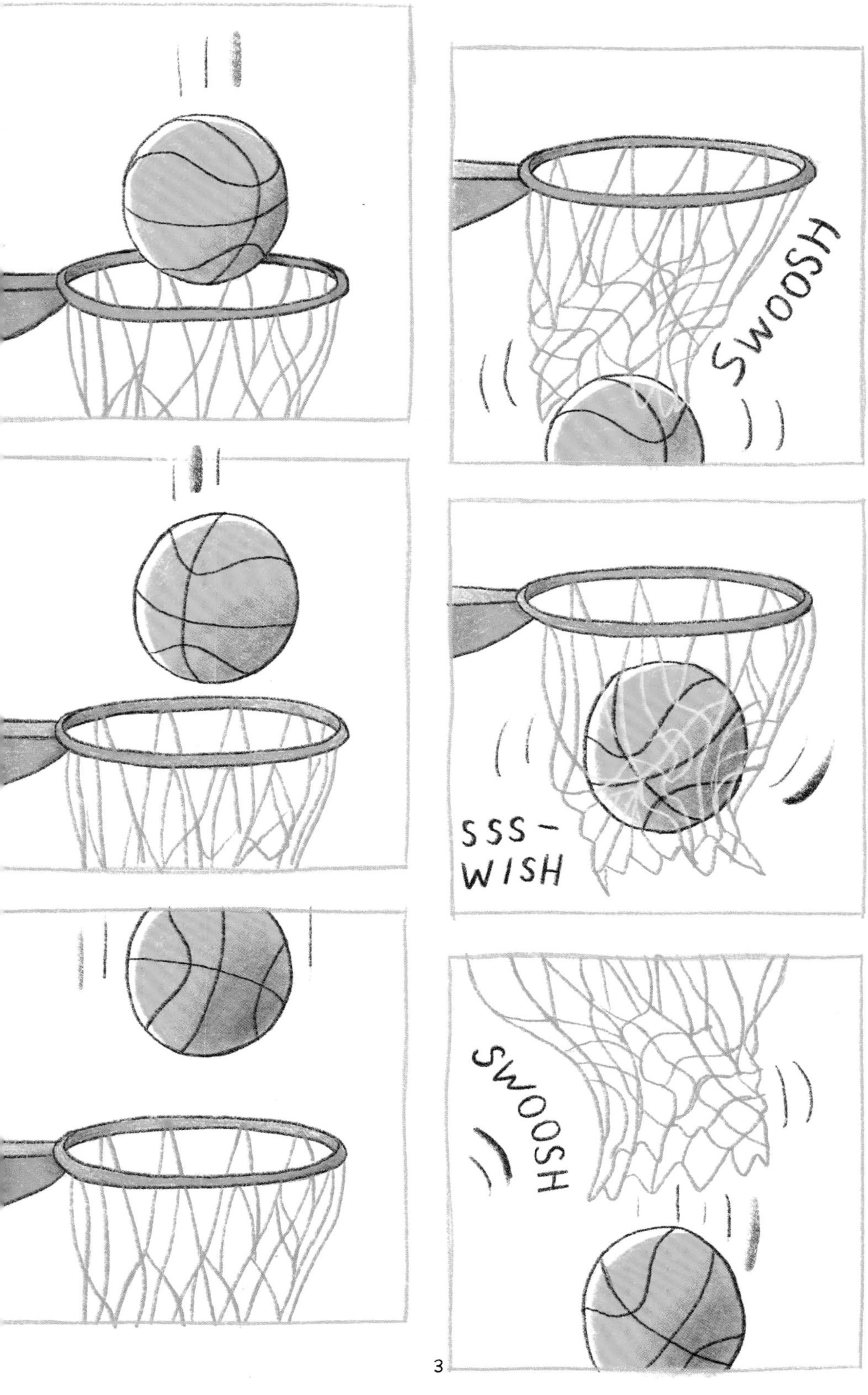
SWOOSH
SSS-
WISH
SWOOSH

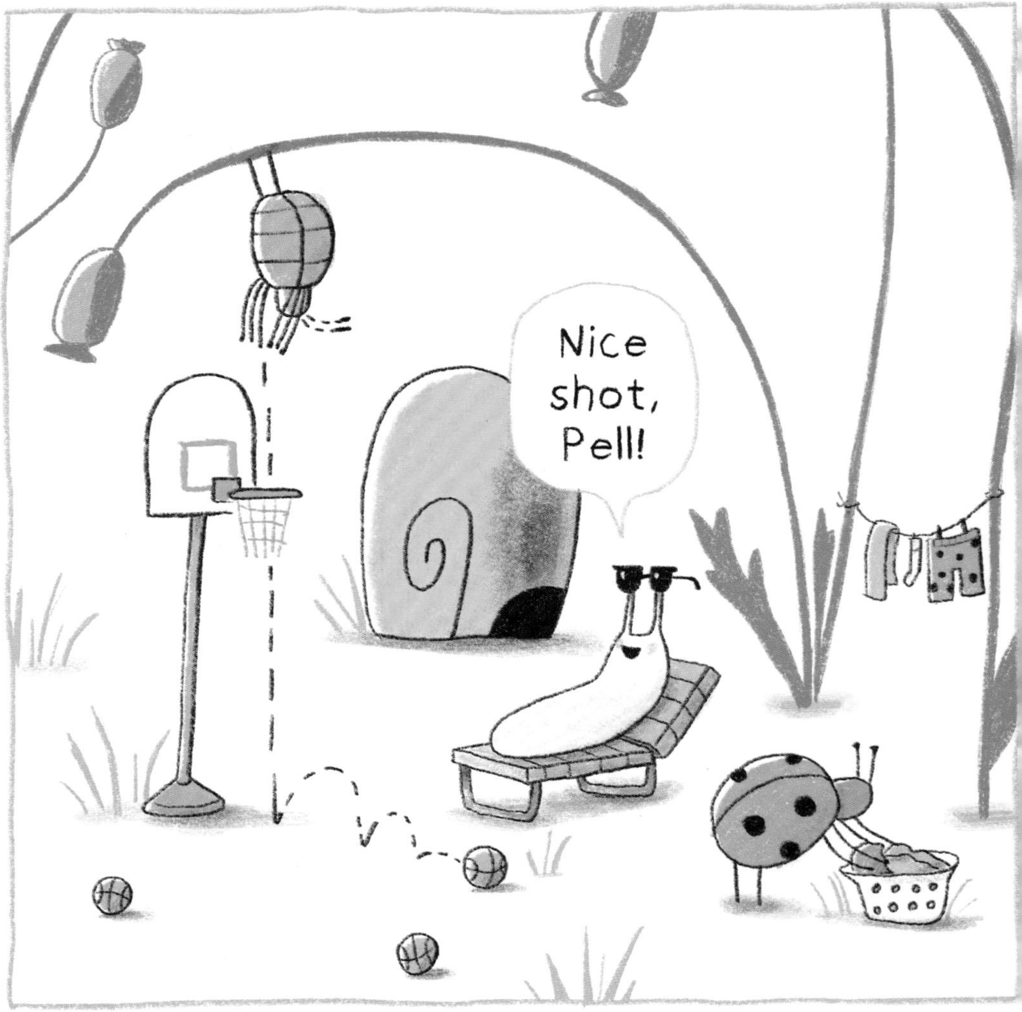
Nice shot, Pell!

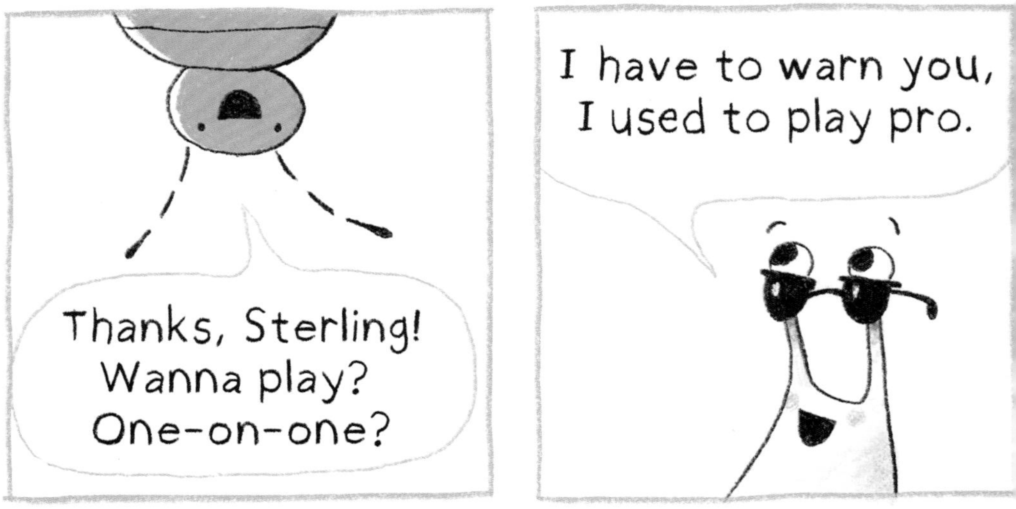
Thanks, Sterling! Wanna play? One-on-one?
I have to warn you, I used to play pro.

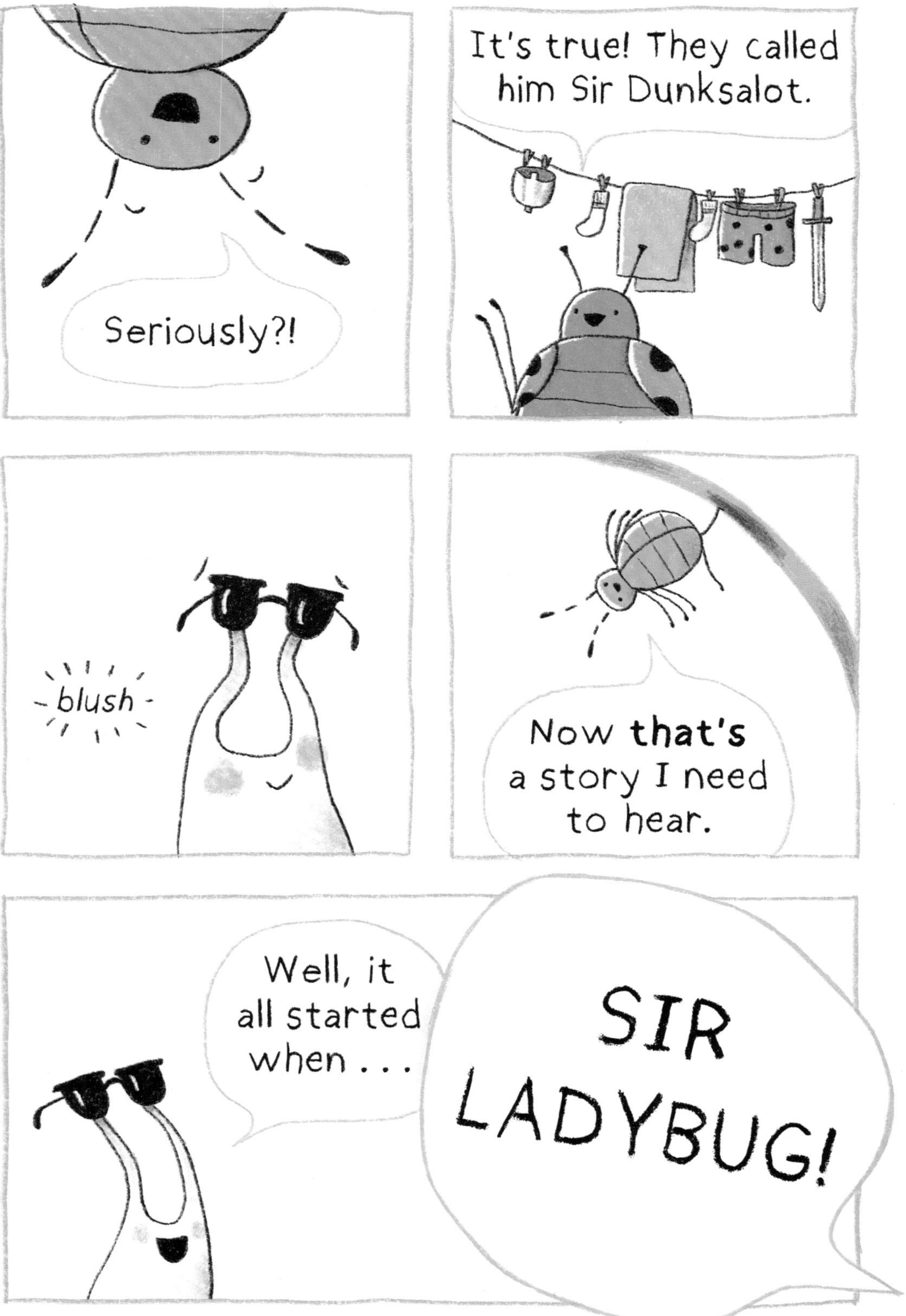
Seriously?!
It's true! They called him Sir Dunksalot.
blush
Now **that's** a story I need to hear.
Well, it all started when . . .
SIR LADYBUG!

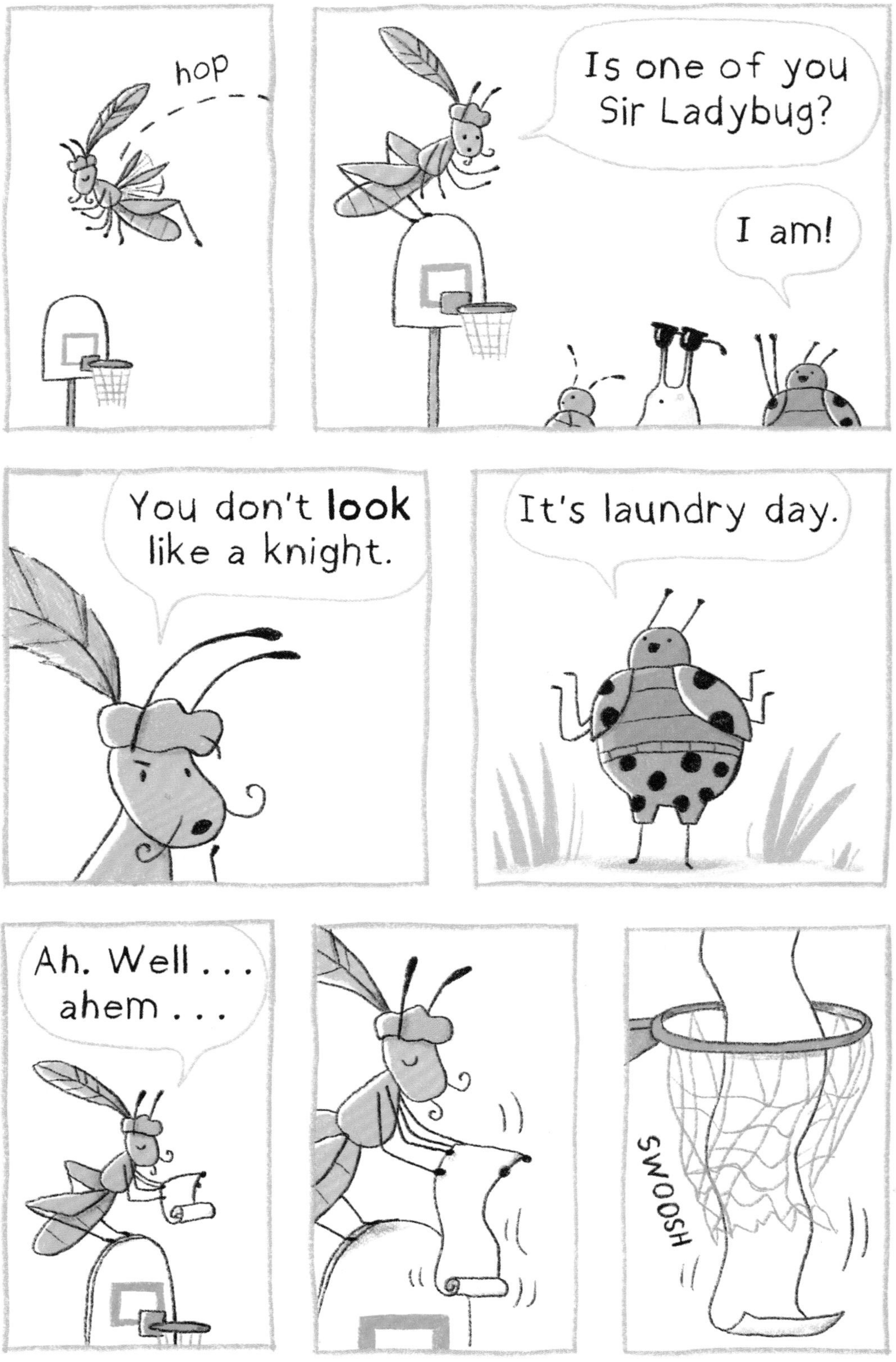
hop
Is one of you Sir Ladybug?
I am!
You don't **look** like a knight.
It's laundry day.
Ah. Well . . . ahem . . .
SWOOSH

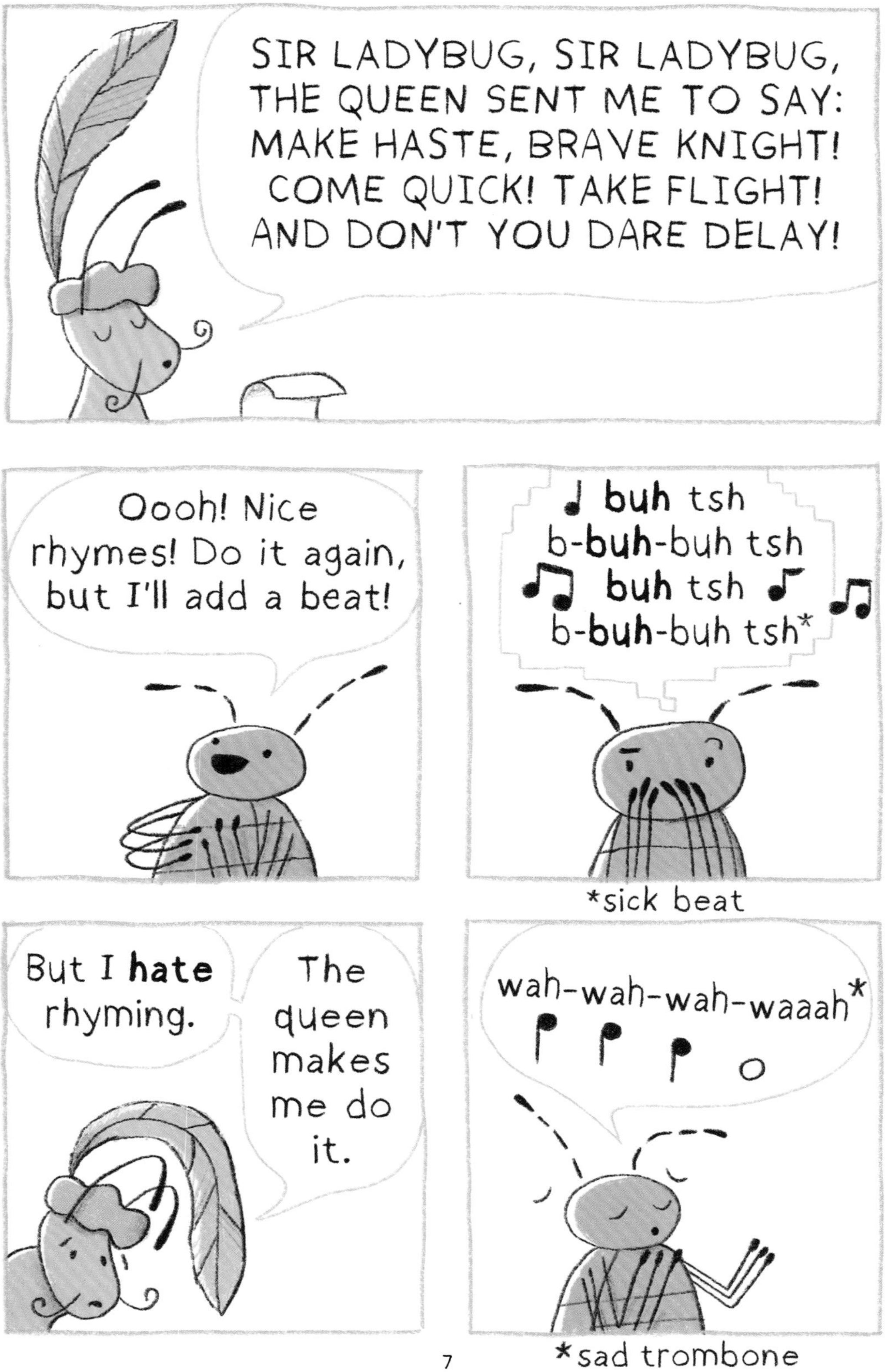
SIR LADYBUG, SIR LADYBUG, THE QUEEN SENT ME TO SAY: MAKE HASTE, BRAVE KNIGHT! COME QUICK! TAKE FLIGHT! AND DON'T YOU DARE DELAY!
Oooh! Nice rhymes! Do it again, but I'll add a beat!
buh tsh b-**buh**-buh tsh **buh** tsh b-**buh**-buh tsh*
*sick beat
But I **hate** rhyming.
The queen makes me do it.
wah-wah-wah-waaah*
*sad trombone

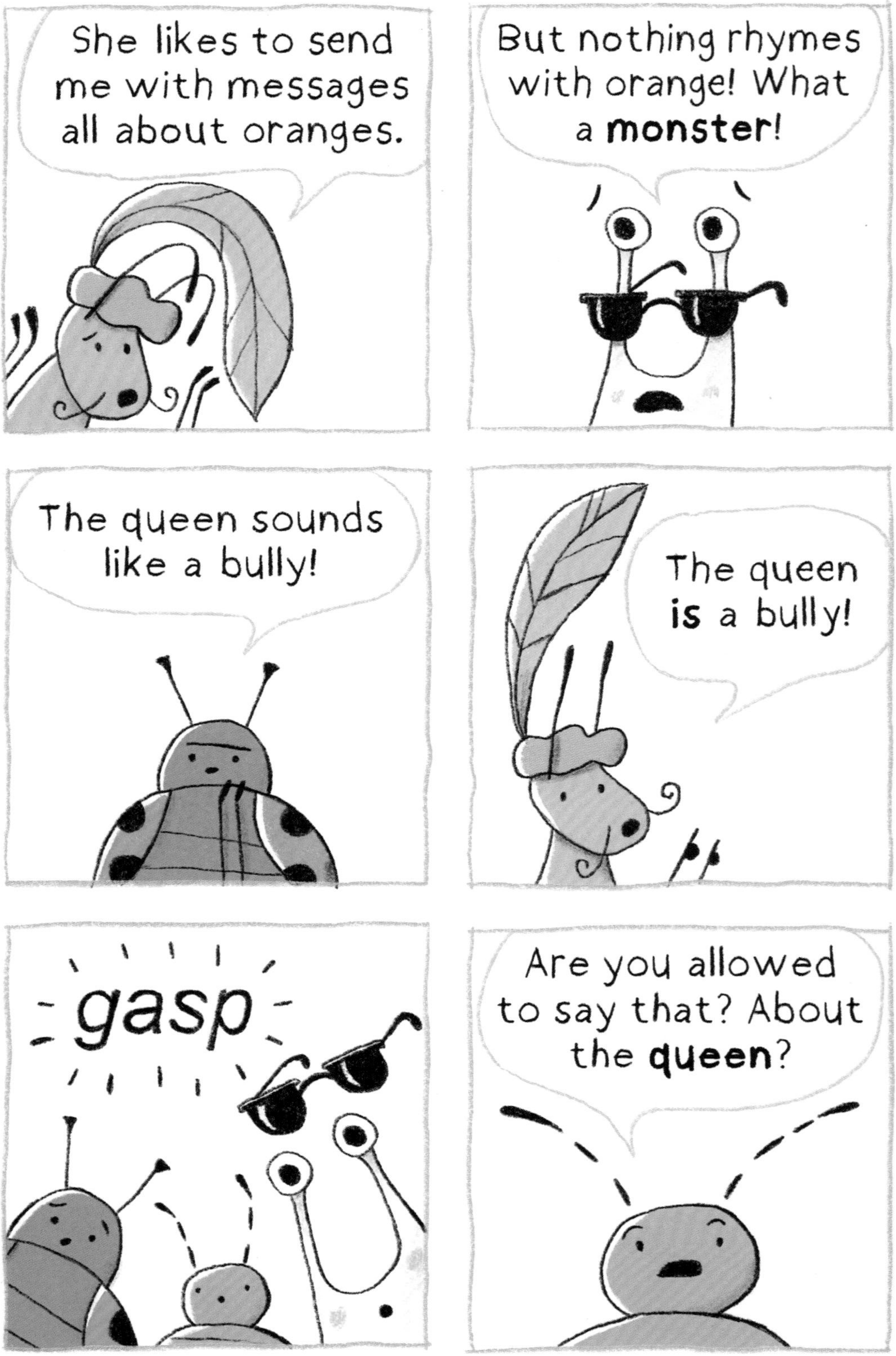
She likes to send me with messages all about oranges.
But nothing rhymes with orange! What a **monster**!
The queen sounds like a bully!
The queen **is** a bully!
gasp
Are you allowed to say that? About the **queen**?

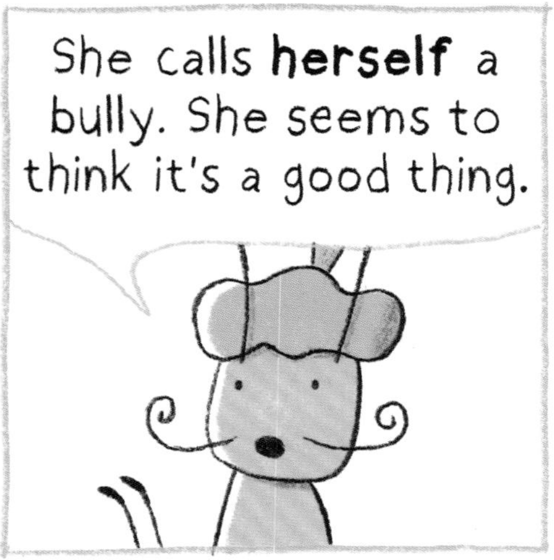
She calls **herself** a bully. She seems to think it's a good thing.

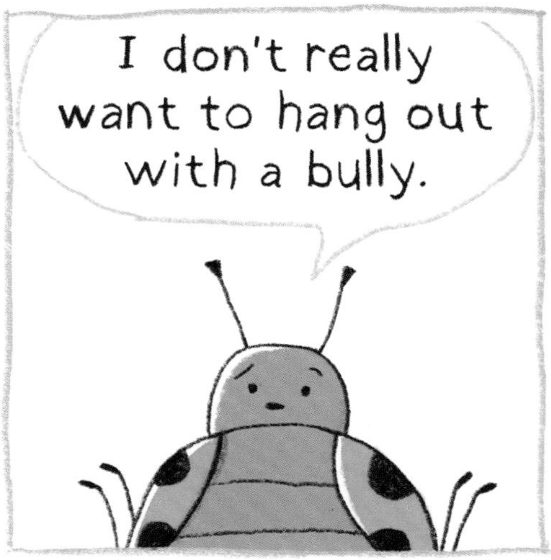
I don't really want to hang out with a bully.

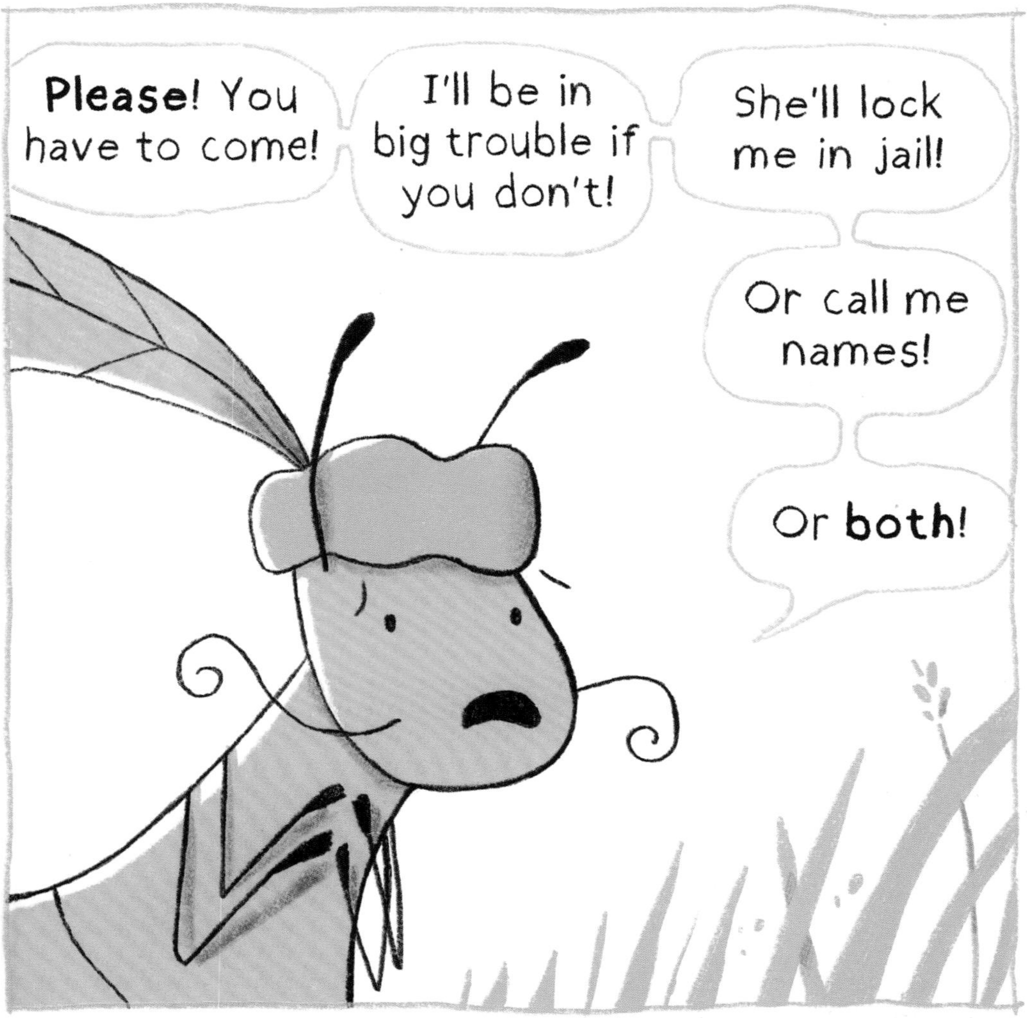
Please! You have to come!
I'll be in big trouble if you don't!
She'll lock me in jail!
Or call me names!
Or **both**!

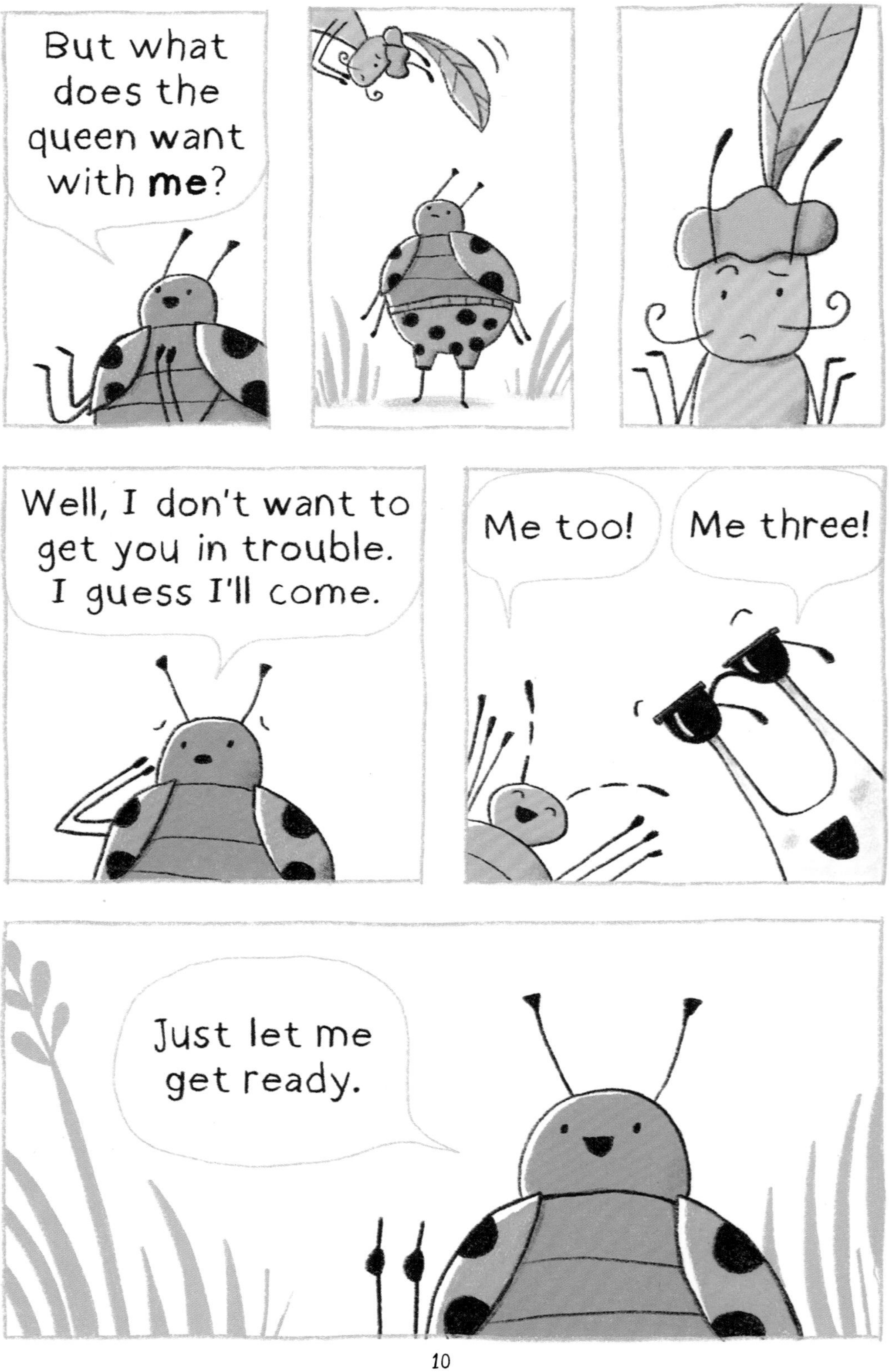
But what does the queen want with **me**?
Well, I don't want to get you in trouble. I guess I'll come.
Me too!
Me three!
Just let me get ready.

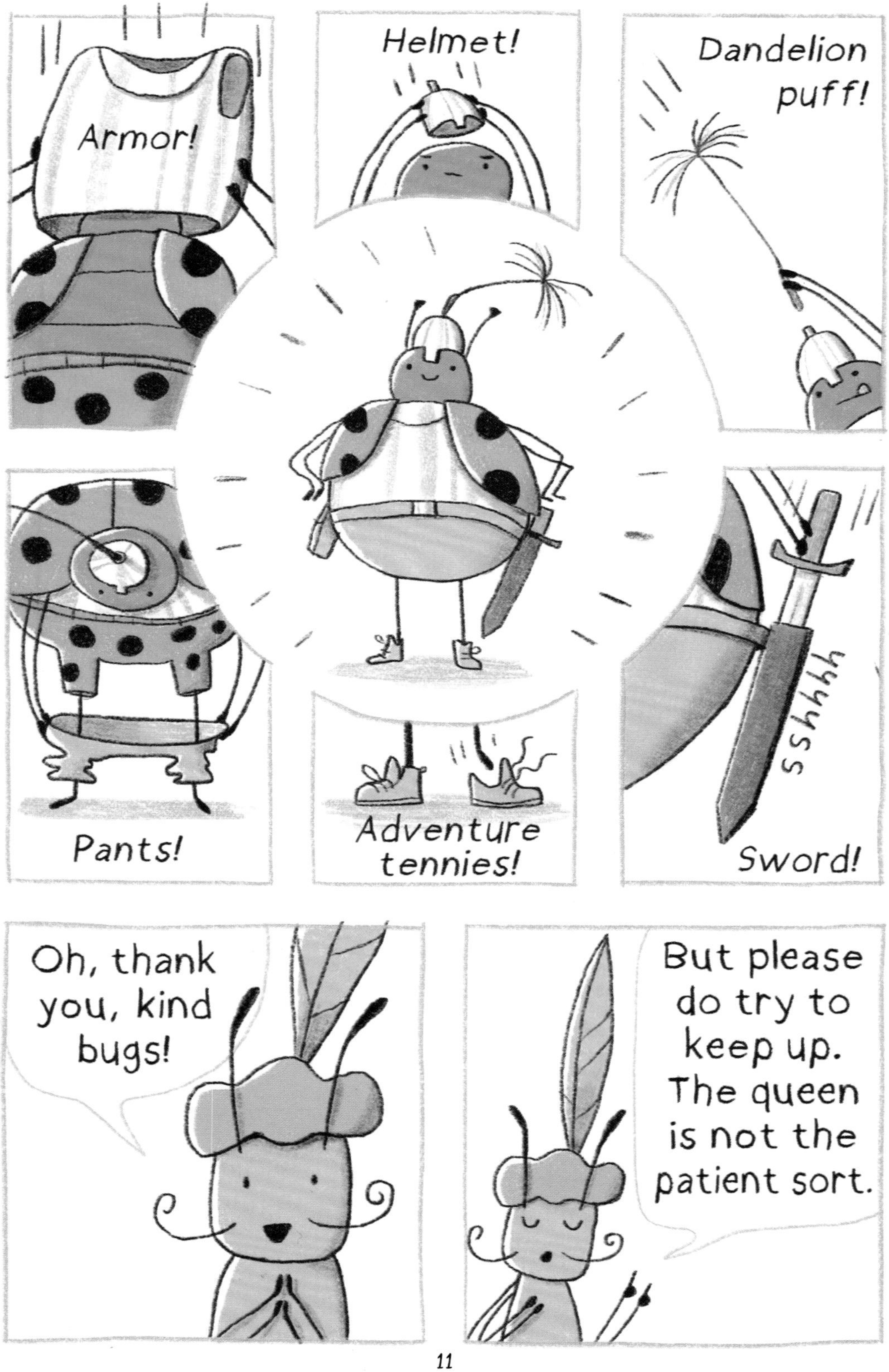
Armor!
Helmet!
Dandelion puff!
Pants!
Adventure tennies!
sshhhh
Sword!
Oh, thank you, kind bugs!
But please do try to keep up. The queen is not the patient sort.

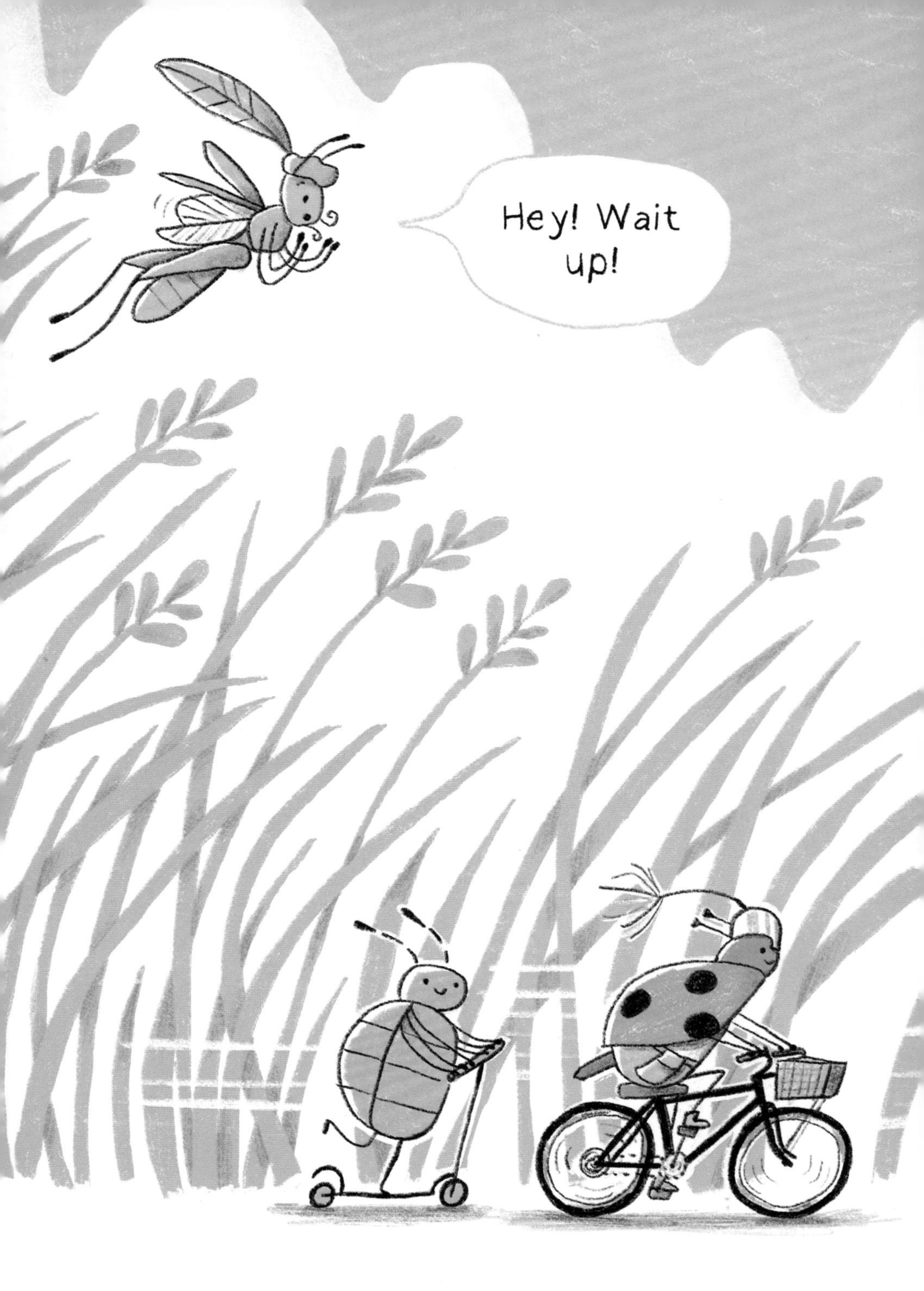
Hey! Wait up!

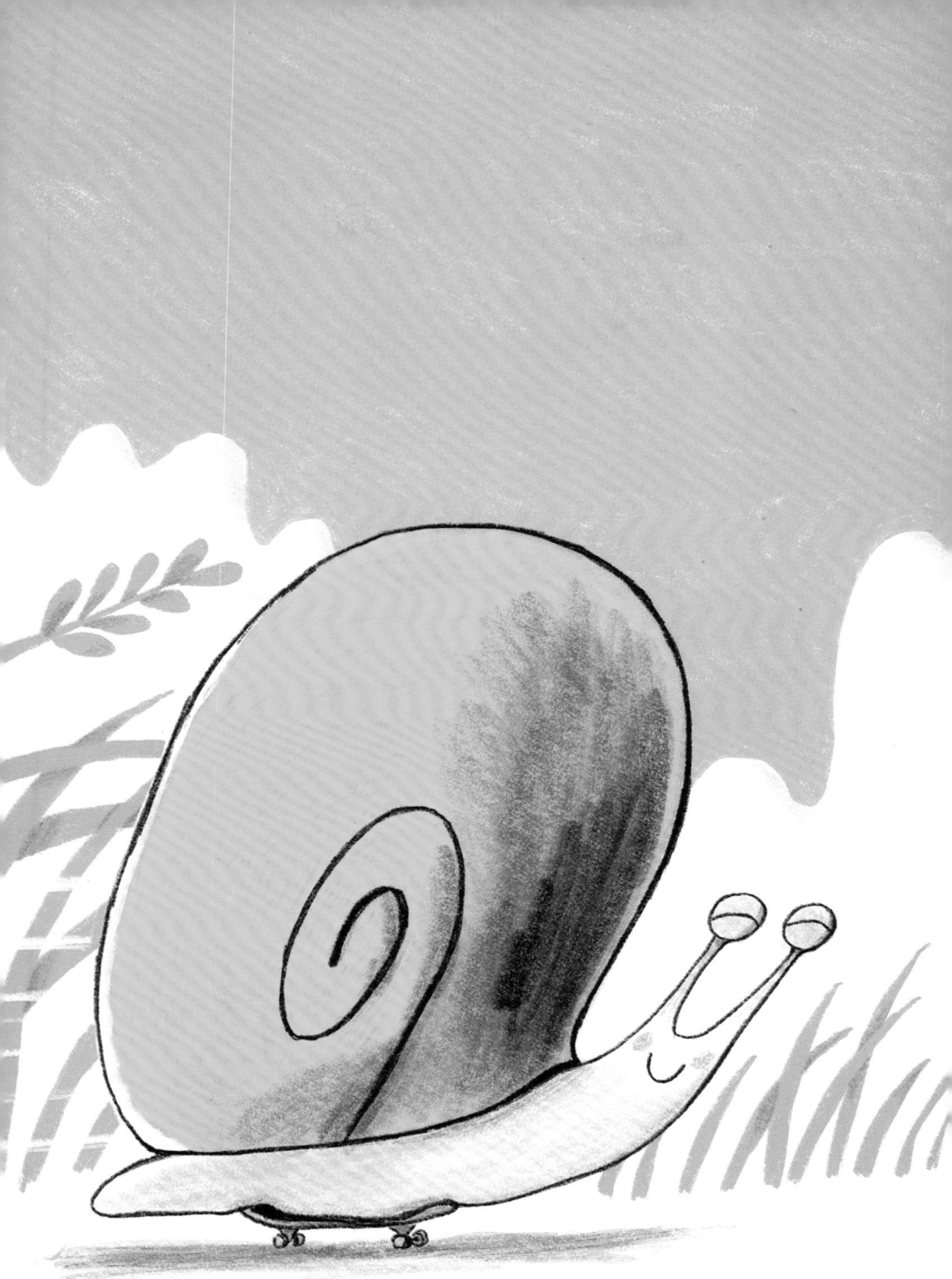

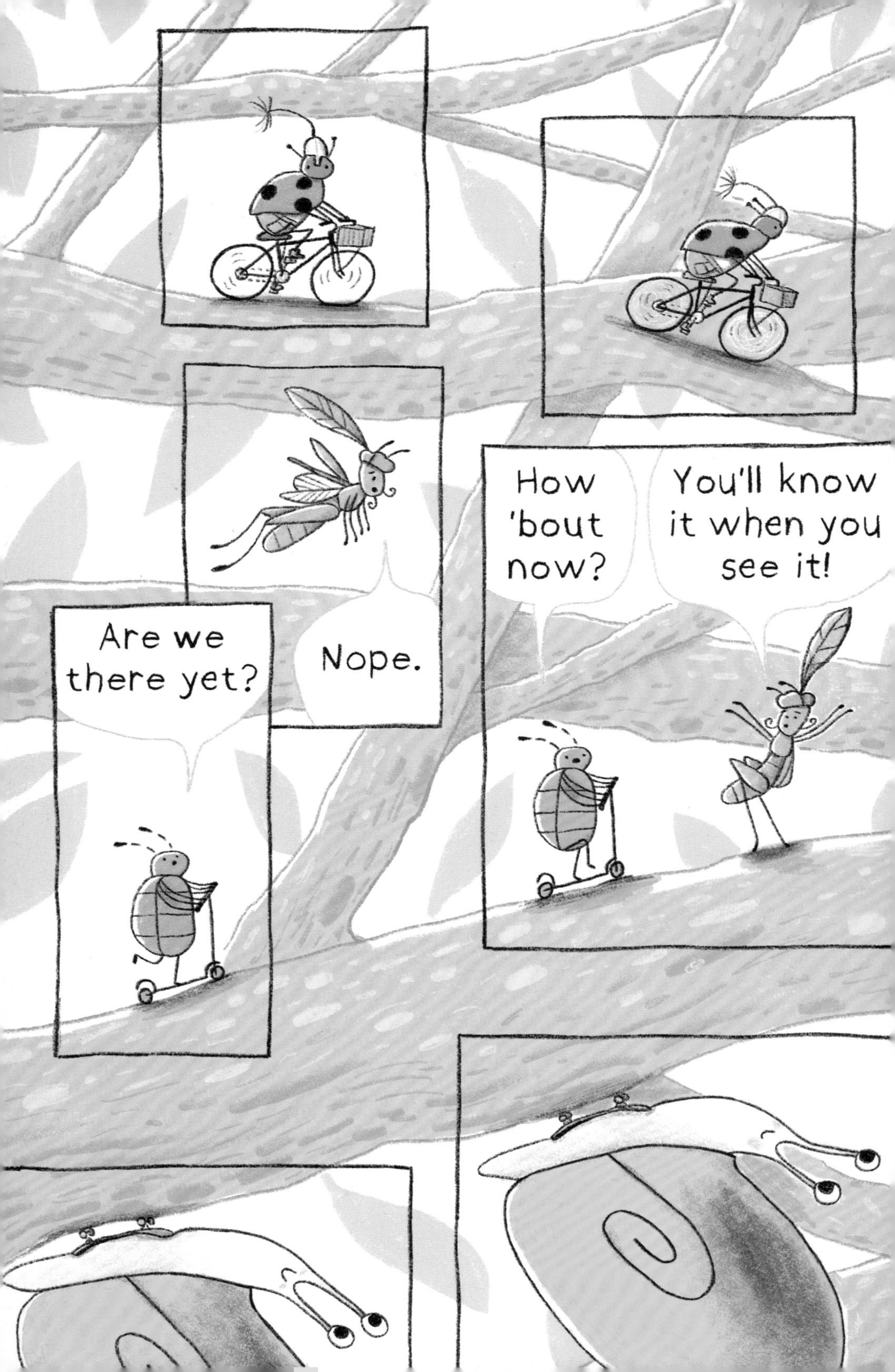

Are we there yet?
Nope.
How 'bout now?
You'll know it when you see it!

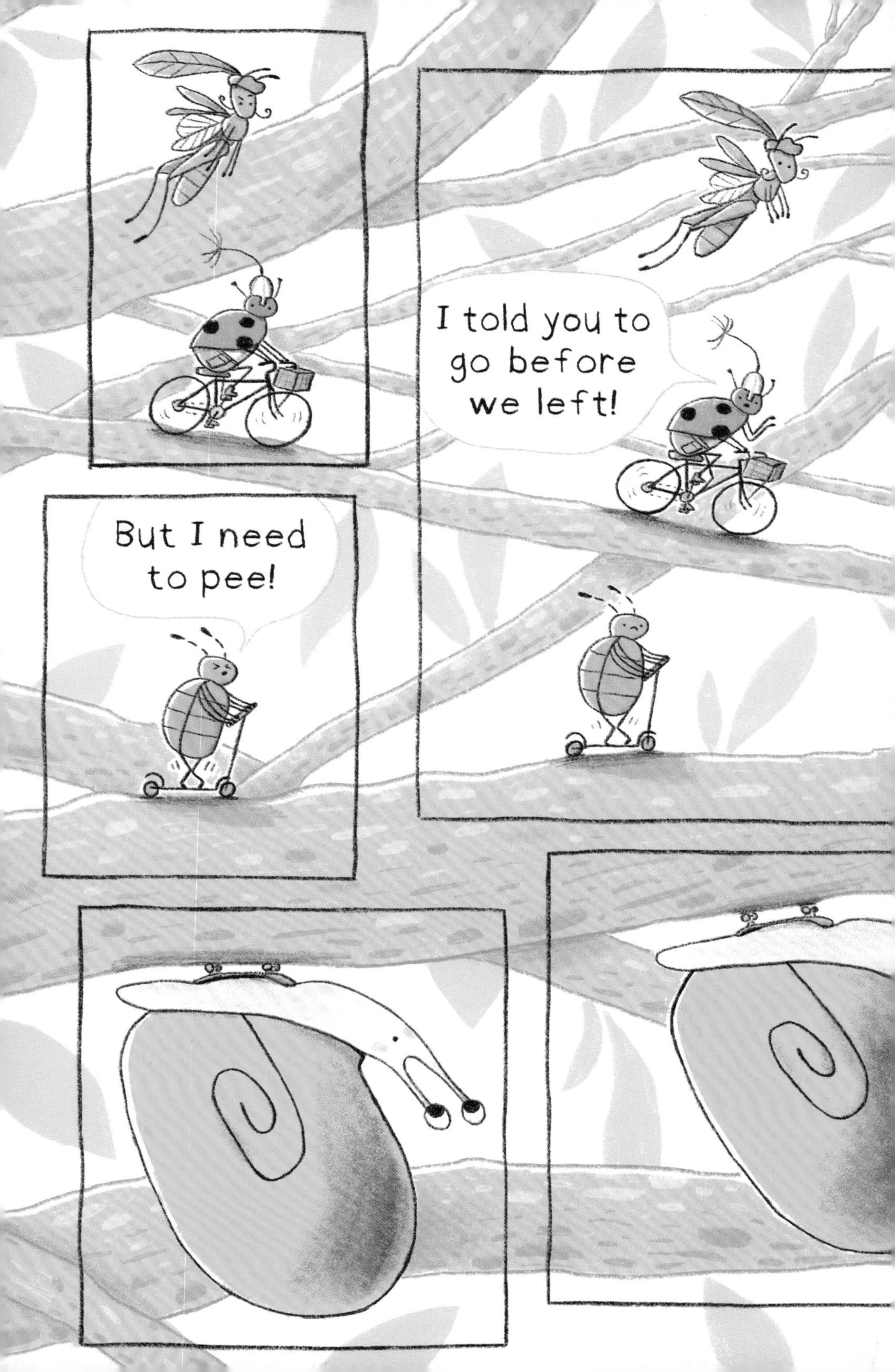
I told you to go before we left!
But I need to pee!

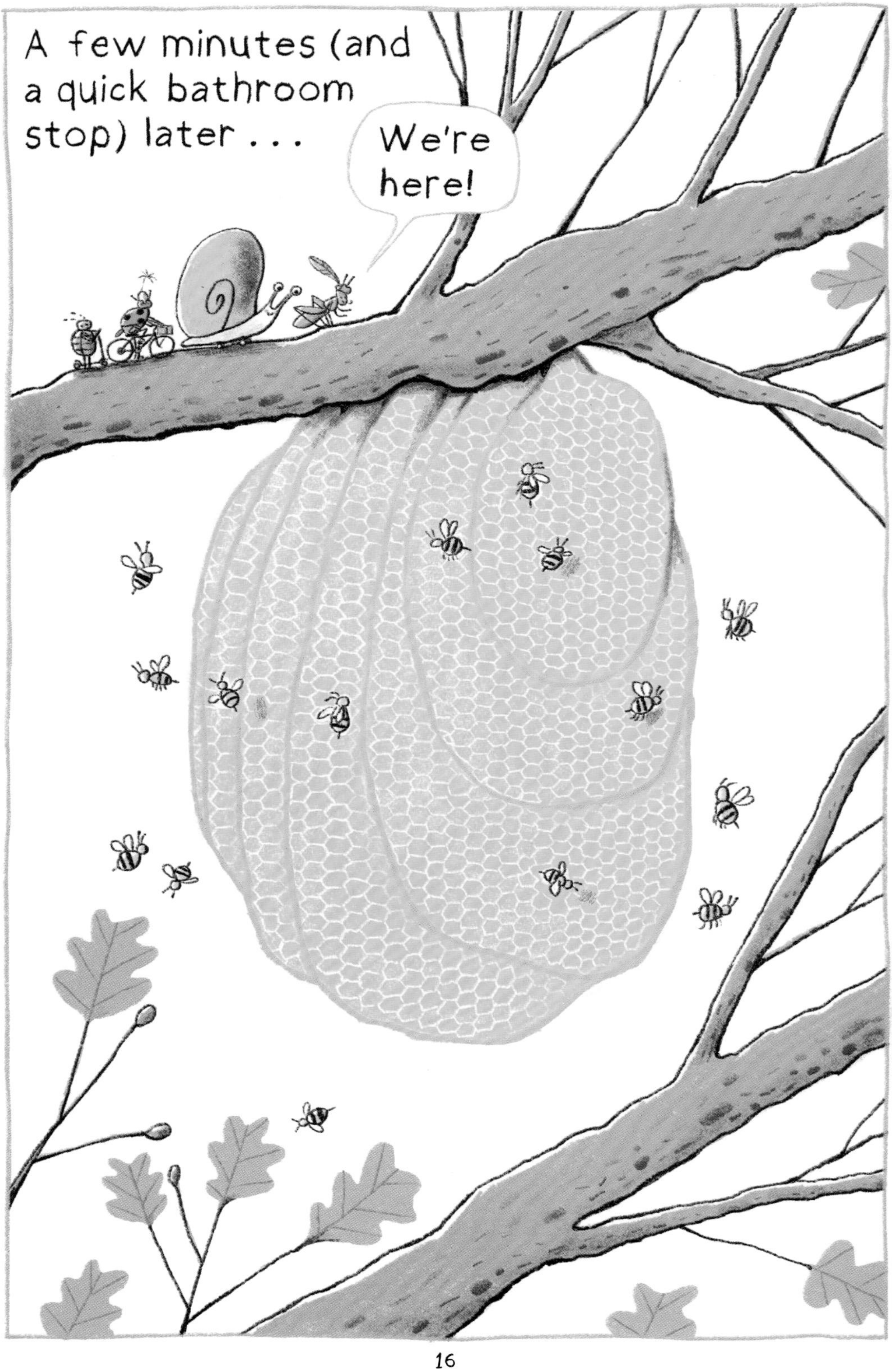
A few minutes (and a quick bathroom stop) later . . .
We're here!

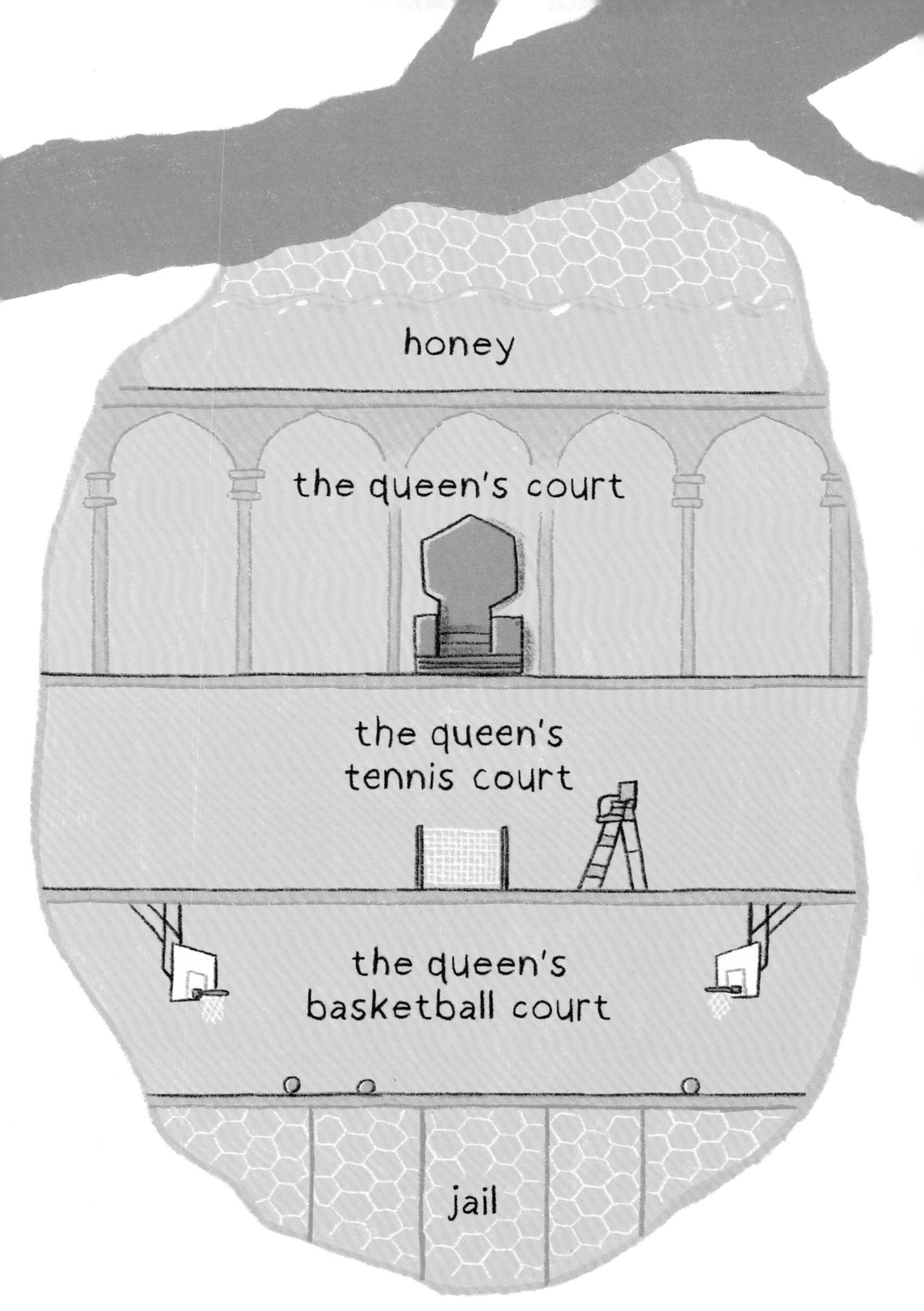
honey
the queen's court
the queen's tennis court
the queen's basketball court
jail

Chapter 2: The Queen

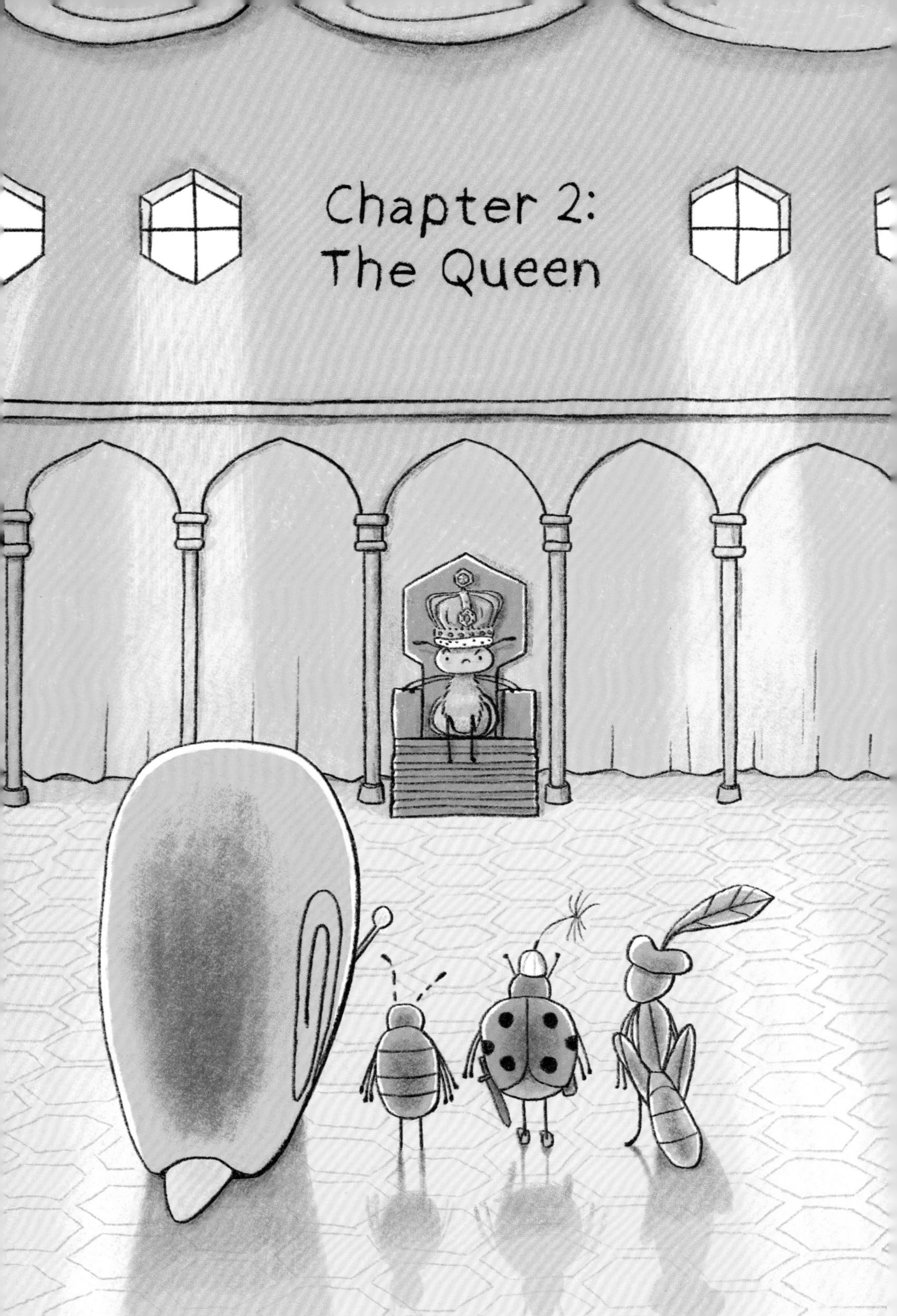

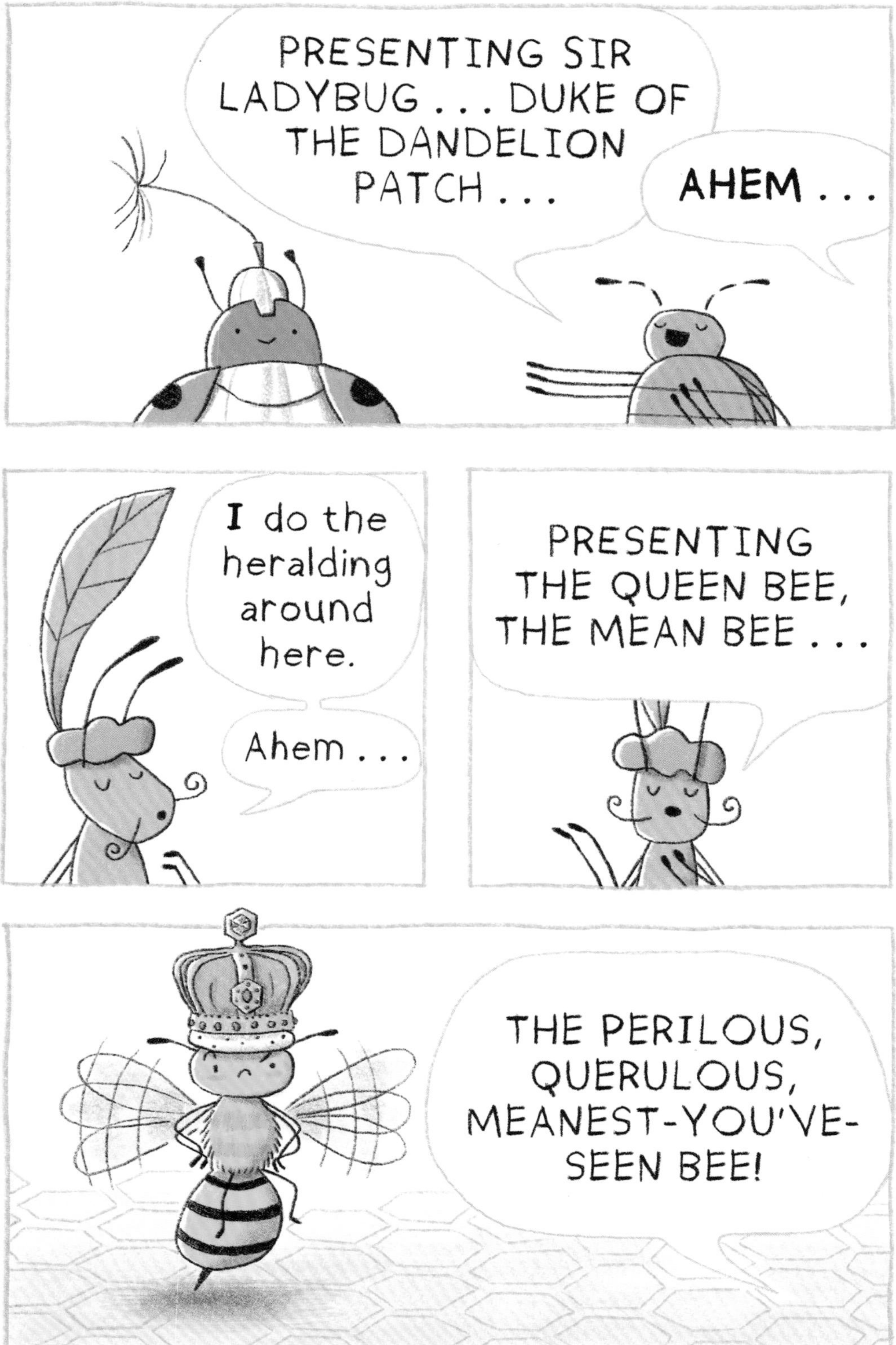
PRESENTING SIR LADYBUG . . . DUKE OF THE DANDELION PATCH . . .
AHEM . . .
I do the heralding around here.
Ahem . . .
PRESENTING THE QUEEN BEE, THE MEAN BEE . . .
THE PERILOUS, QUERULOUS, MEANEST-YOU'VE-SEEN BEE!

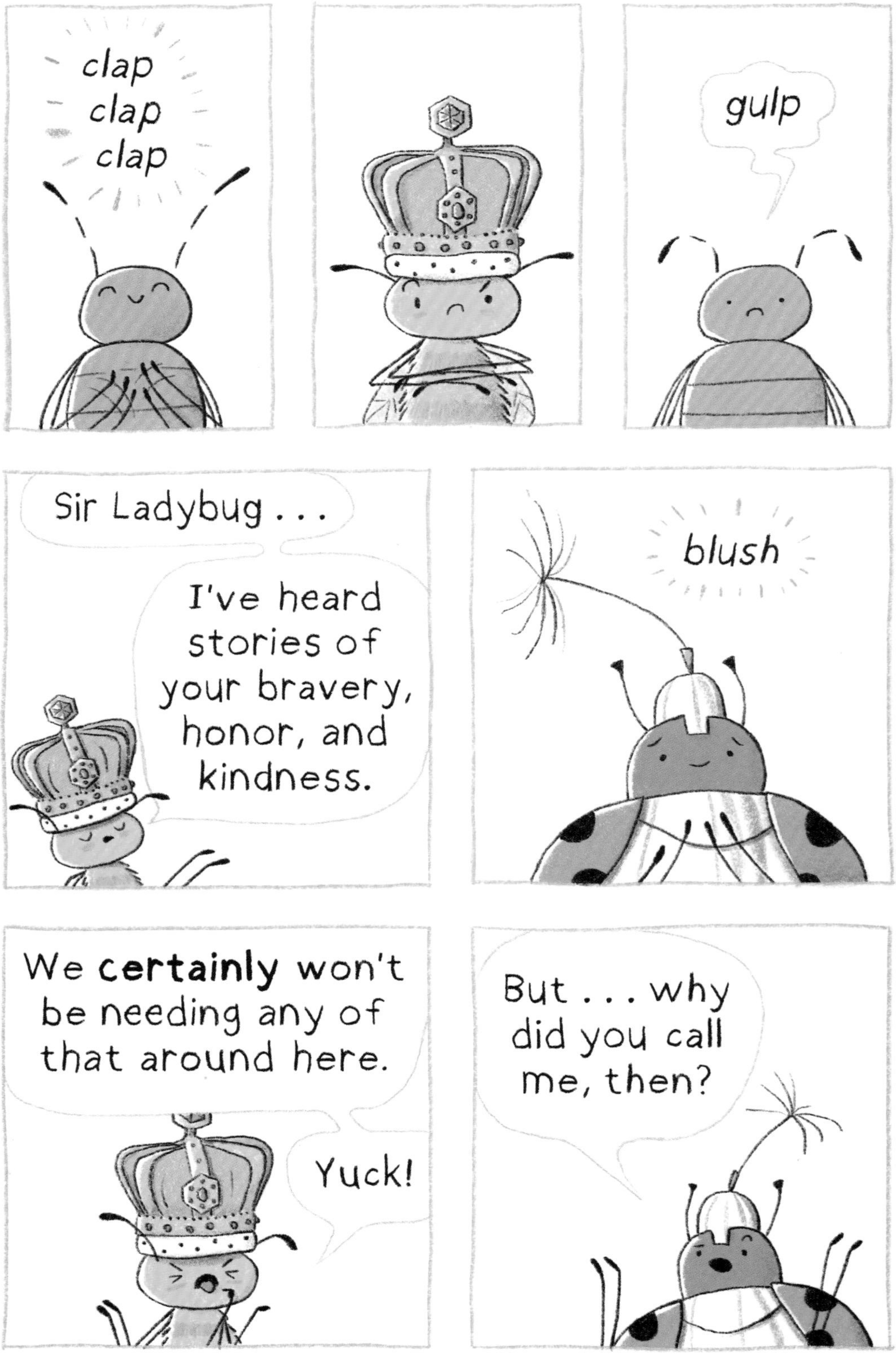
clap
clap
clap
gulp
Sir Ladybug . . .
I've heard stories of your bravery, honor, and kindness.
blush
We **certainly** won't be needing any of that around here.
Yuck!
But . . . why did you call me, then?

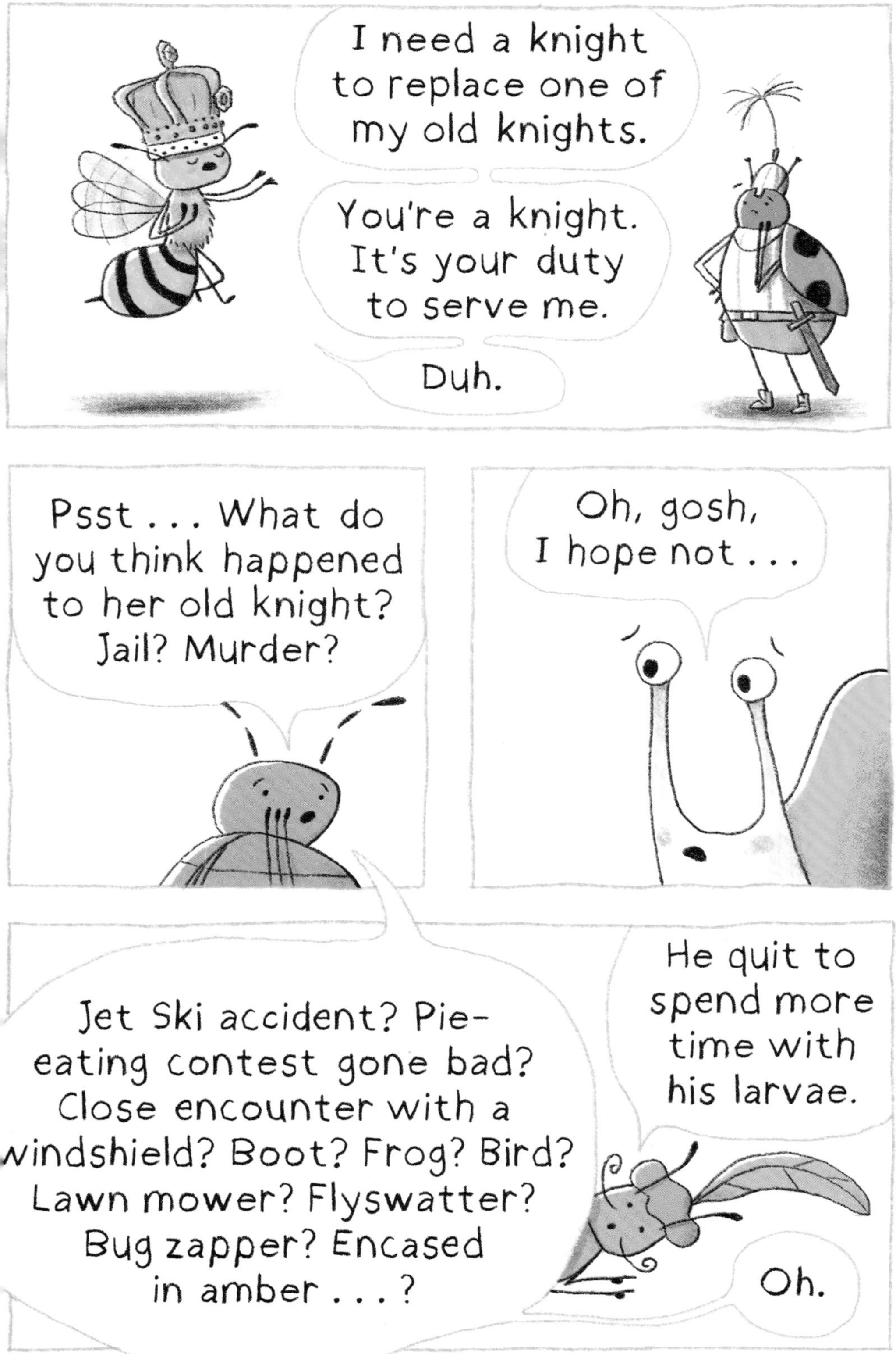
I need a knight to replace one of my old knights.
You're a knight. It's your duty to serve me.
Duh.
Psst . . . What do you think happened to her old knight? Jail? Murder?
Oh, gosh, I hope not . . .
Jet Ski accident? Pie-eating contest gone bad? Close encounter with a windshield? Boot? Frog? Bird? Lawn mower? Flyswatter? Bug zapper? Encased in amber . . . ?
He quit to spend more time with his larvae.
Oh.

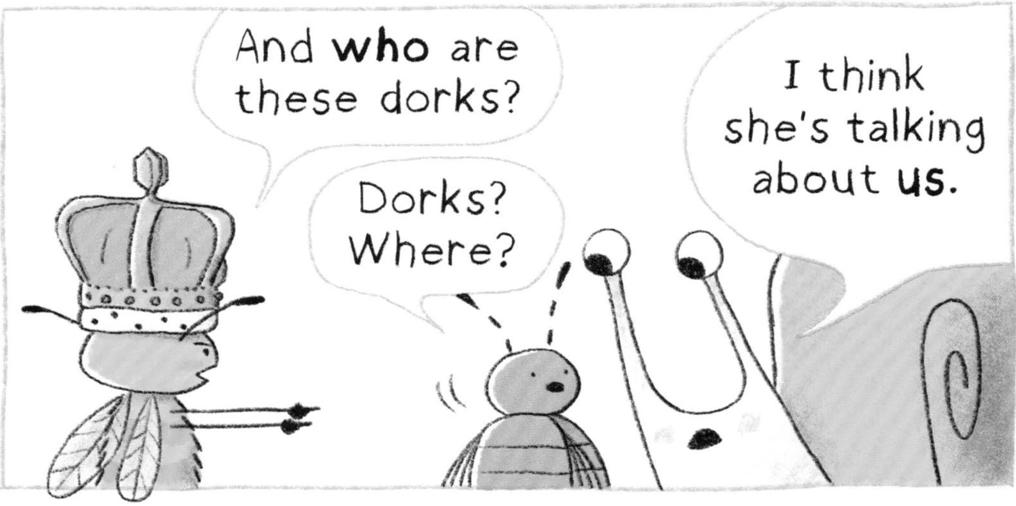
And **who** are these dorks?
Dorks? Where?
I think she's talking about **us**.

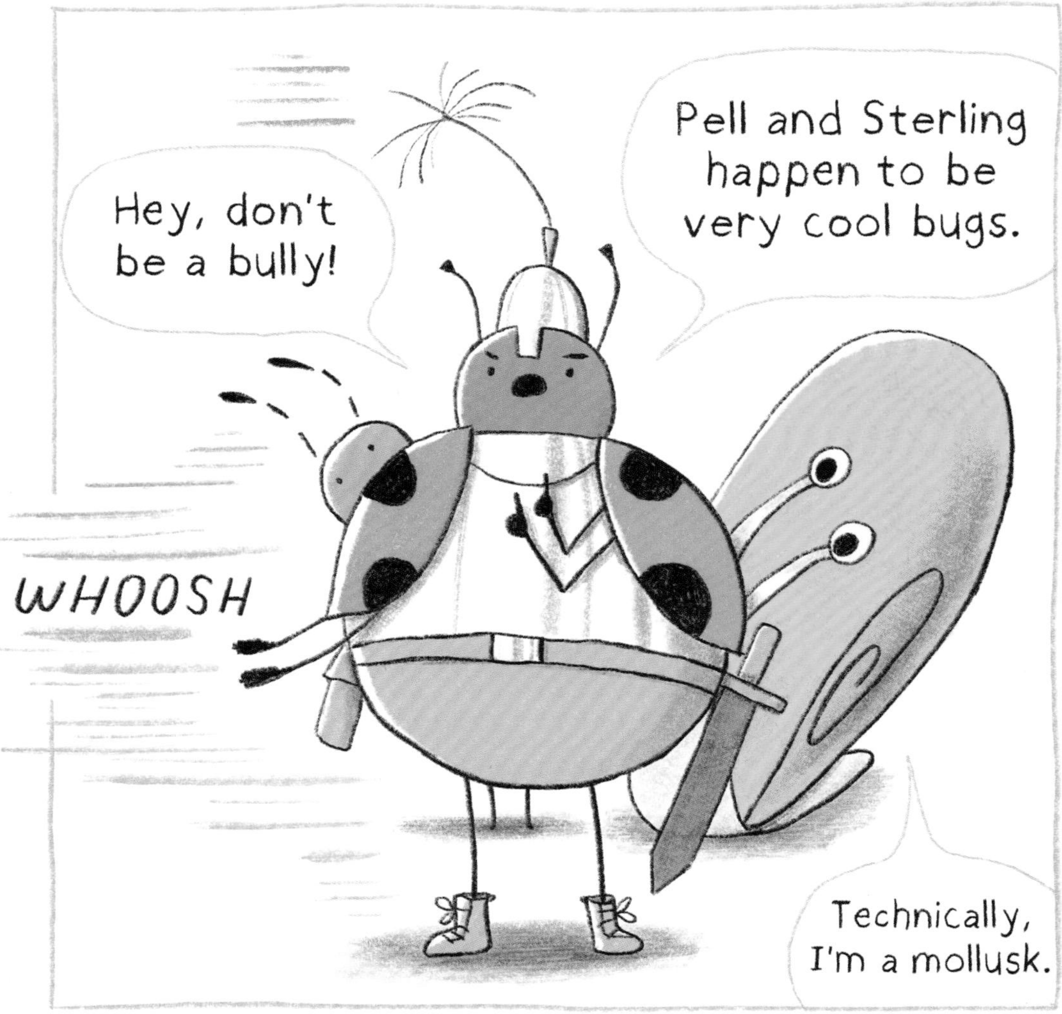
Hey, don't be a bully!
Pell and Sterling happen to be very cool bugs.
WHOOSH
Technically, I'm a mollusk.

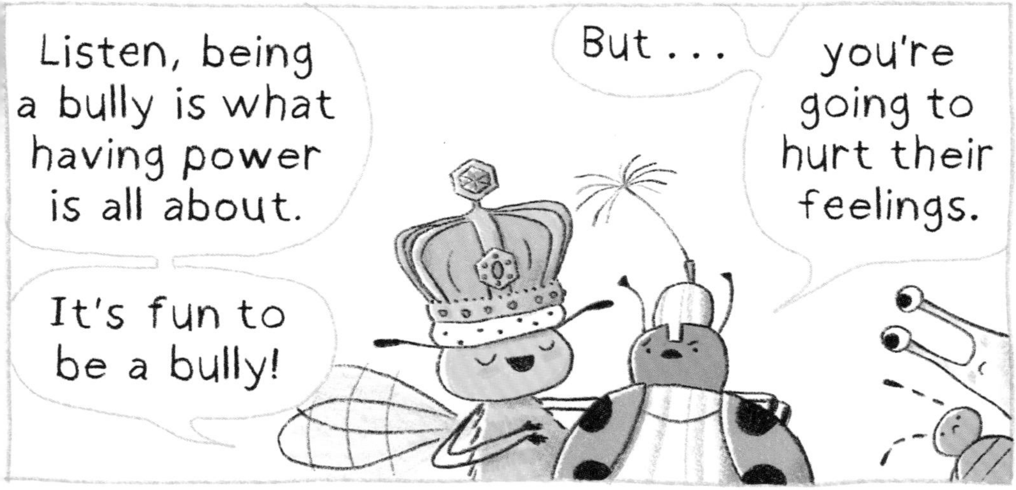
Listen, being a bully is what having power is all about.
It's fun to be a bully!
But . . .
you're going to hurt their feelings.

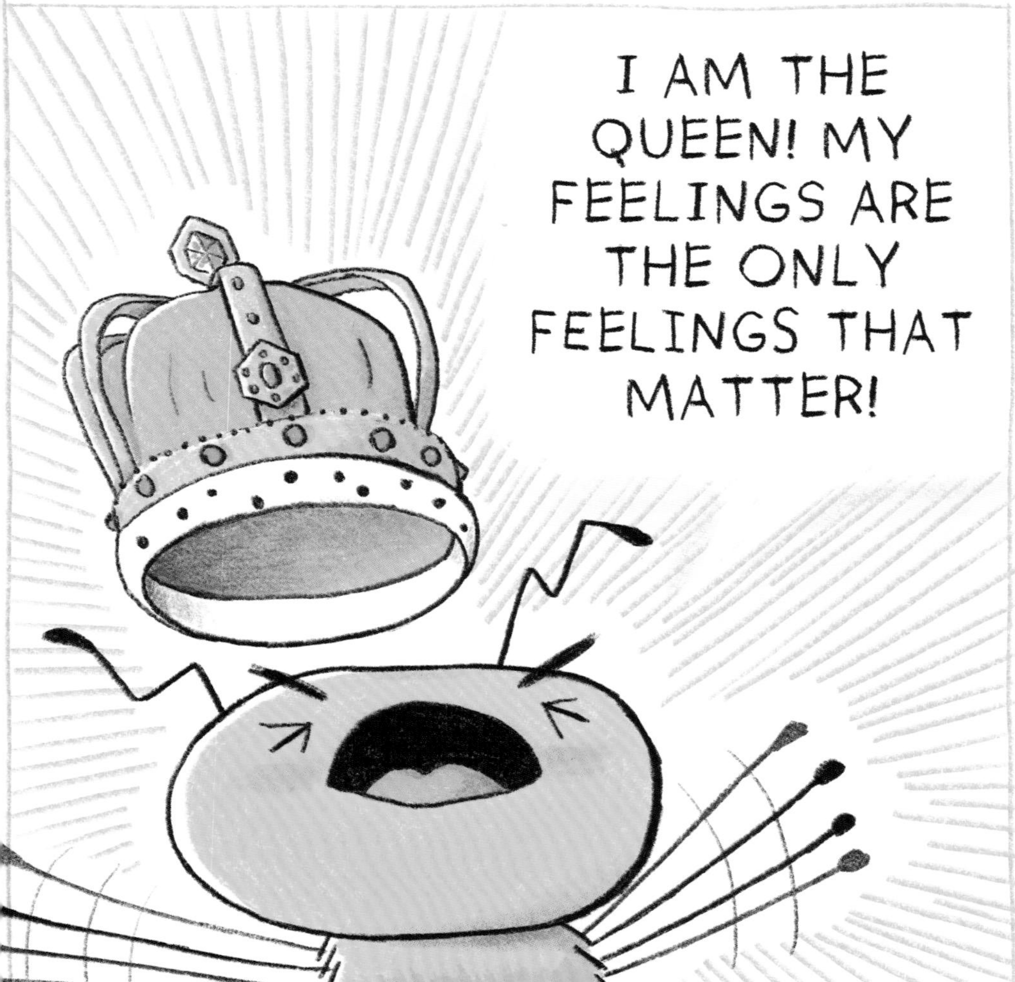
I AM THE QUEEN! MY FEELINGS ARE THE ONLY FEELINGS THAT MATTER!

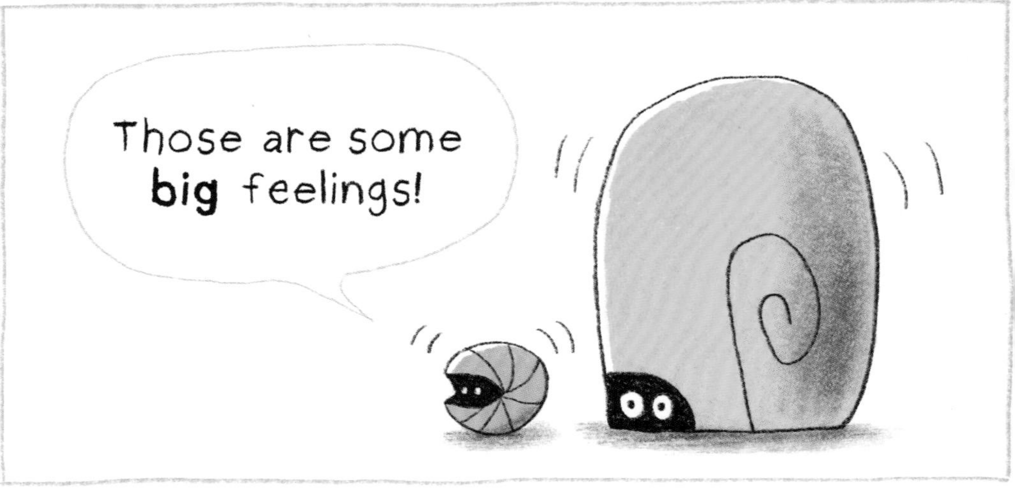
Those are some **big** feelings!

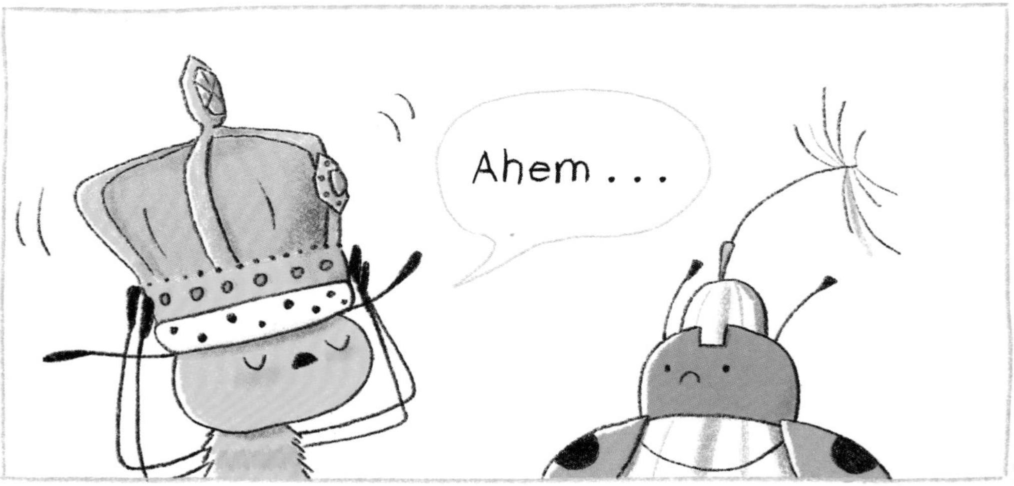
Ahem . . .

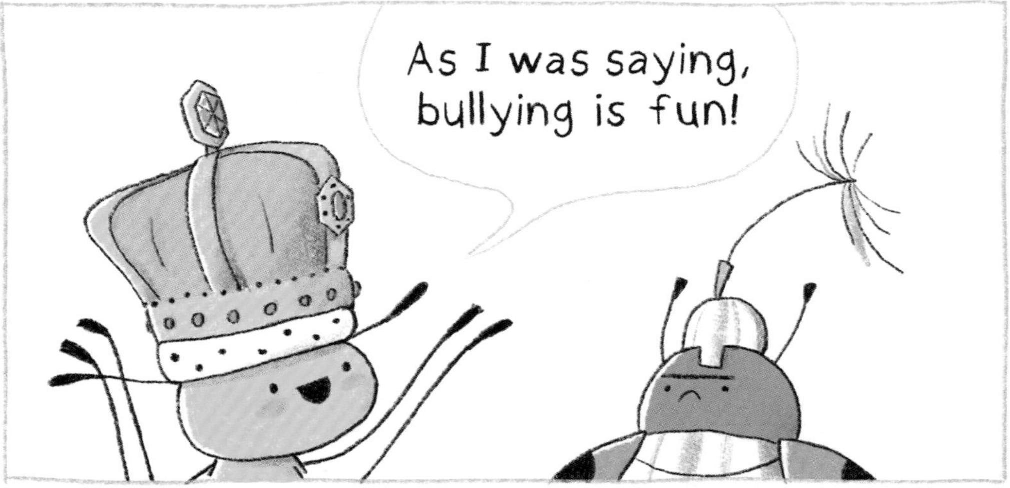
As I was saying, bullying is fun!

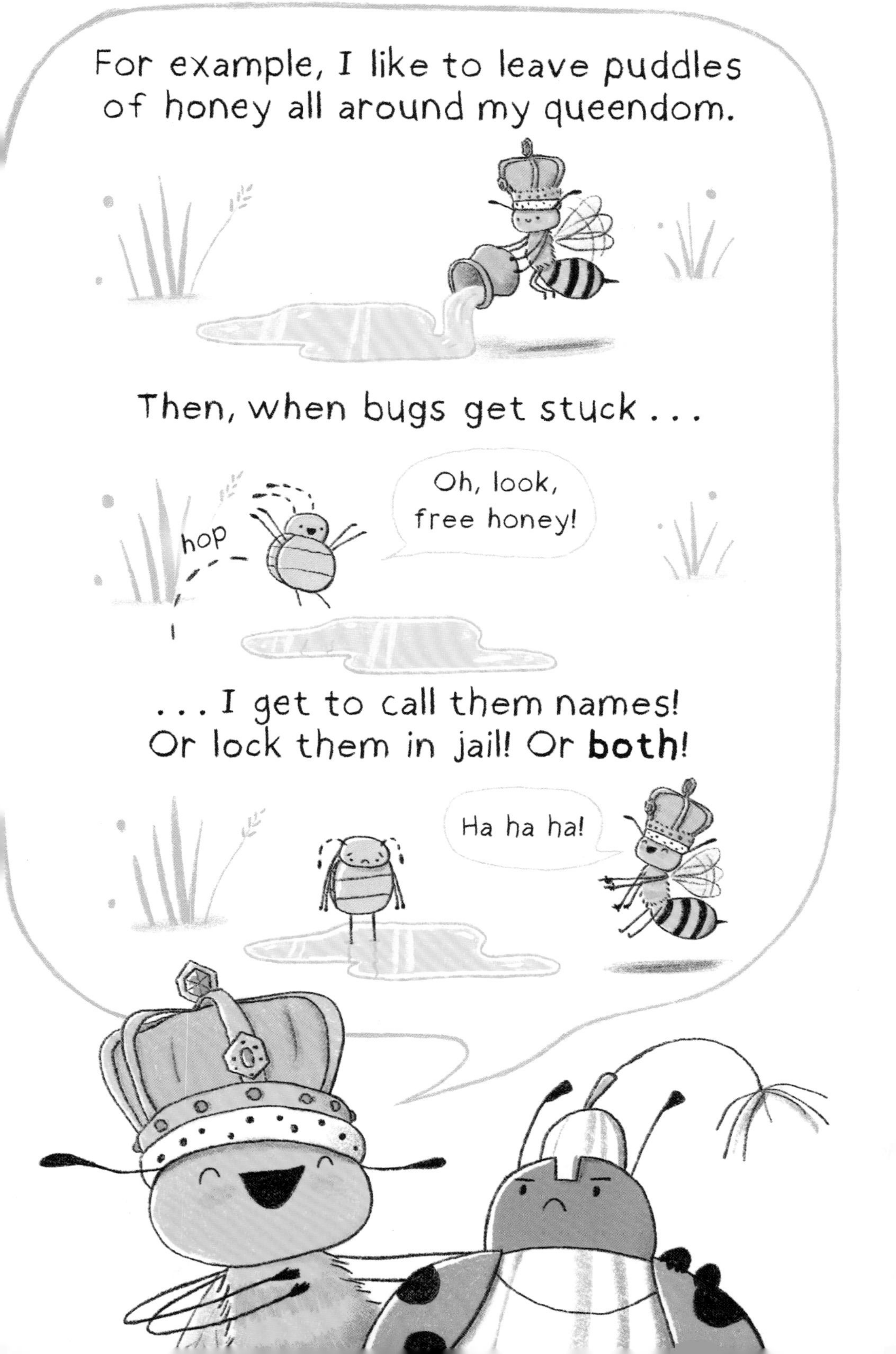
For example, I like to leave puddles of honey all around my queendom.
Then, when bugs get stuck . . .
hop
Oh, look, free honey!
. . . I get to call them names! Or lock them in jail! Or **both**!
Ha ha ha!

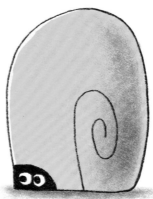

That doesn't sound fun. That sounds mean.

I think it sounds like a cry for help.

GUARDS! ARREST THESE DORKS!

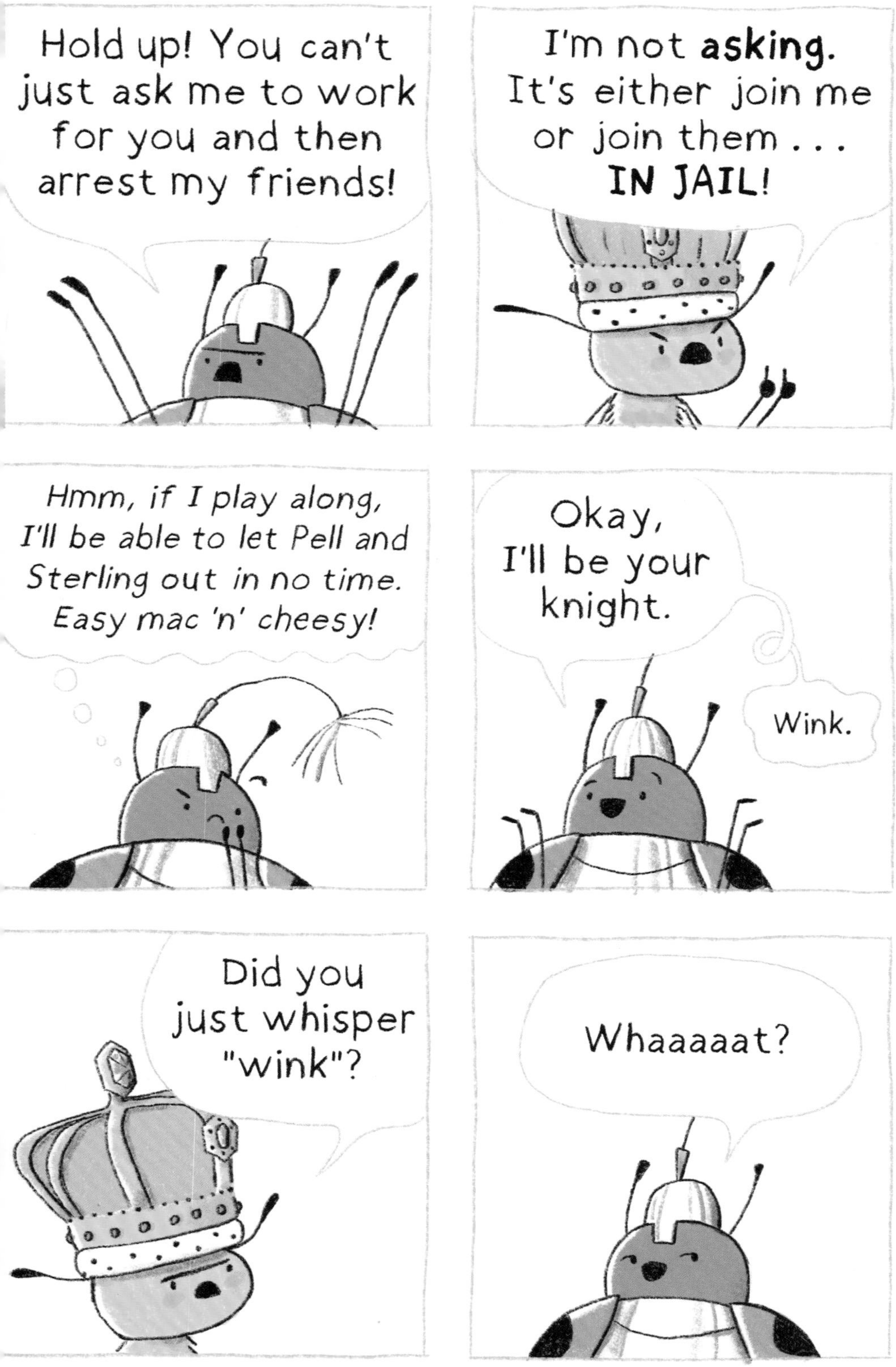
Hold up! You can't just ask me to work for you and then arrest my friends!
I'm not **asking.** It's either join me or join them . . . **IN JAIL!**
Hmm, if I play along, I'll be able to let Pell and Sterling out in no time. Easy mac 'n' cheesy!
Okay, I'll be your knight.
Wink.
Did you just whisper "wink"?
Whaaaaat?

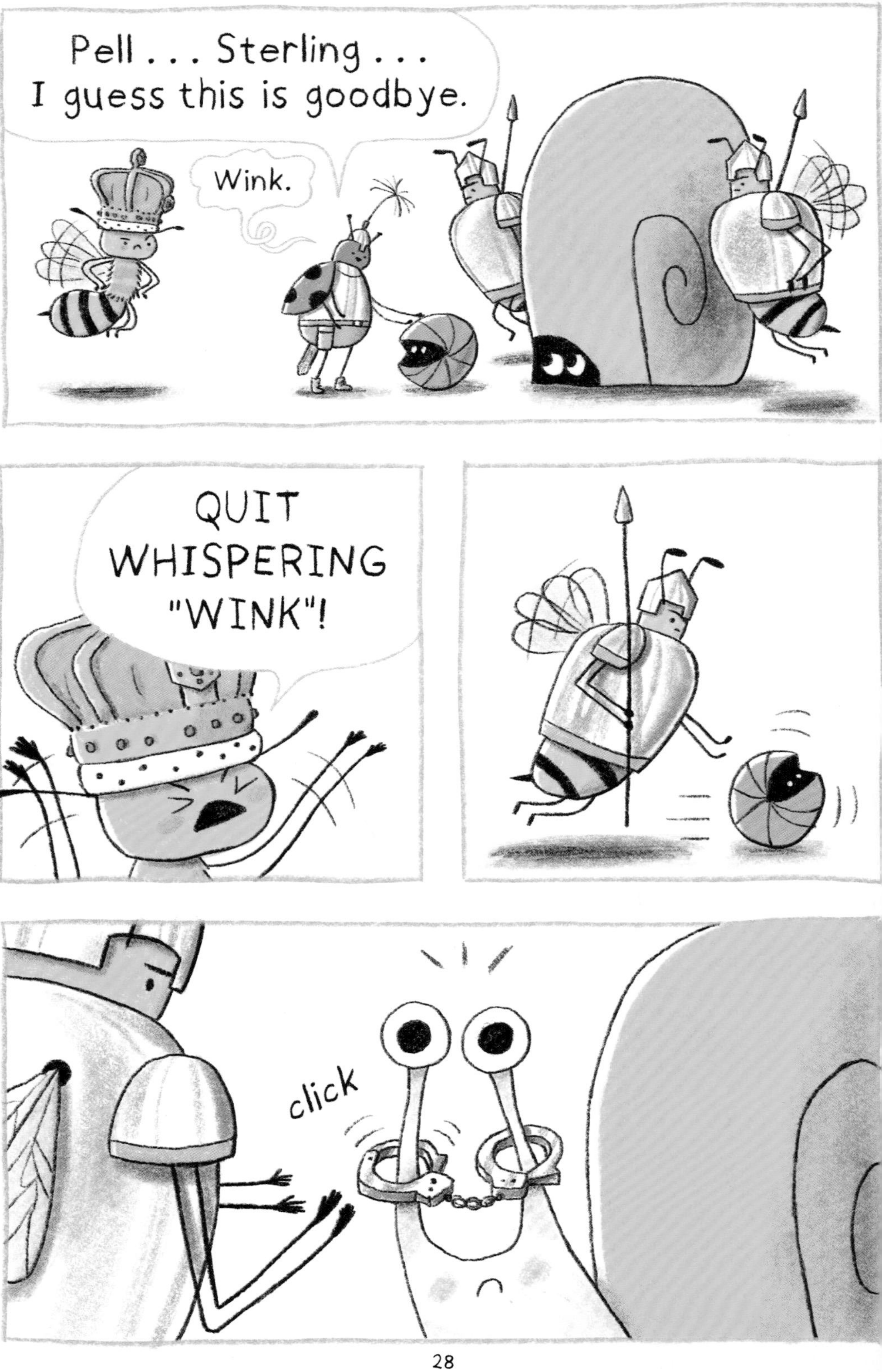
Pell . . . Sterling . . .
I guess this is goodbye.
Wink.
QUIT WHISPERING "WINK"!
click

To be continued . . .

(after these words from
our sponsors)

Advertisements

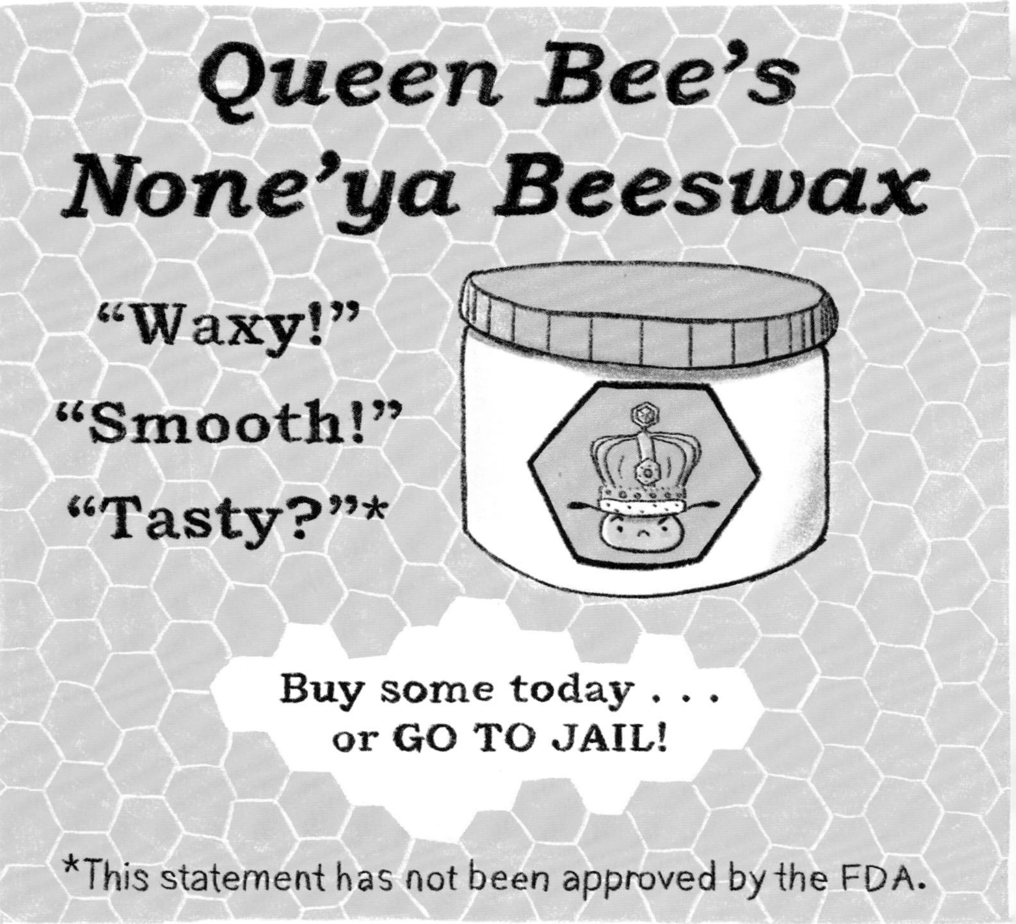
Queen Bee's
None'ya Beeswax
"Waxy!"
"Smooth!"
"Tasty?"*
Buy some today . . .
or GO TO JAIL!
*This statement has not been approved by the FDA.

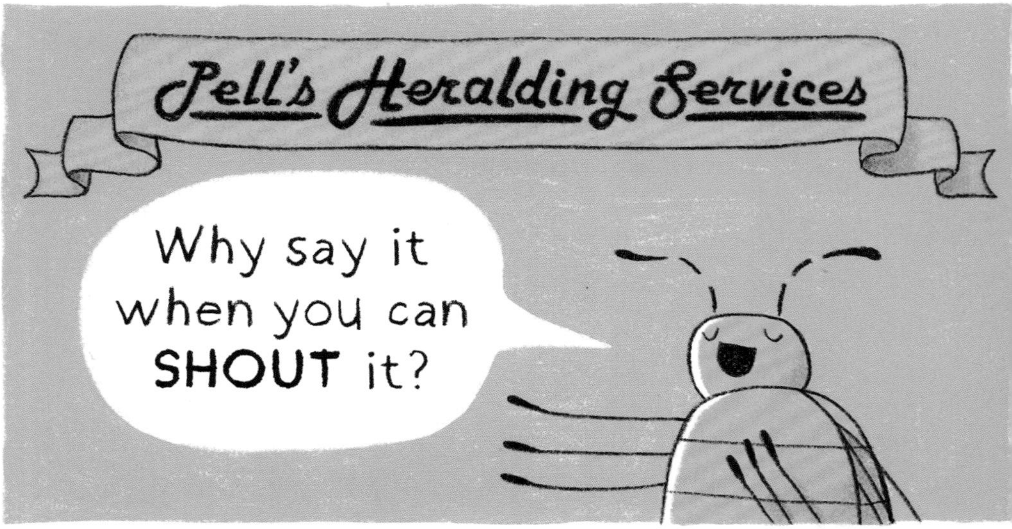
Pell's Heralding Services
Why say it when you can SHOUT it?

Advertisements

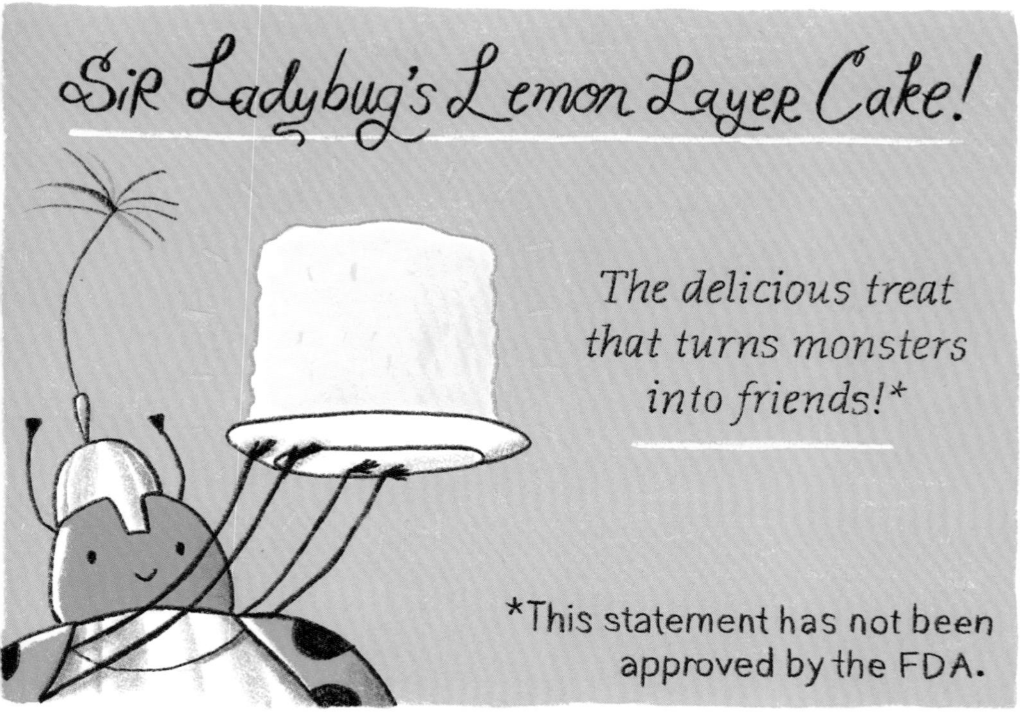

Sir Ladybug's Lemon Layer Cake!
The delicious treat that turns monsters into friends!*
*This statement has not been approved by the FDA.

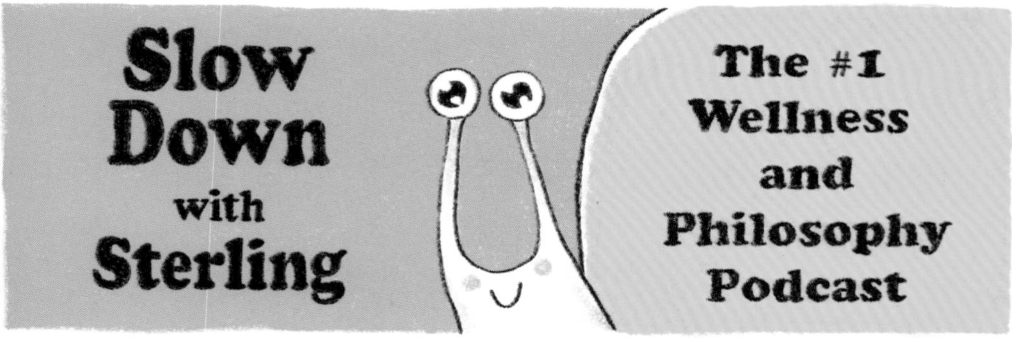

Slow Down with Sterling
The #1 Wellness and Philosophy Podcast

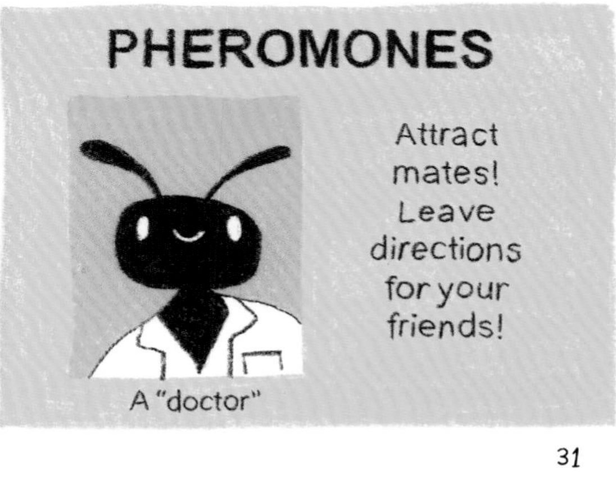

PHEROMONES
Attract mates! Leave directions for your friends!
A "doctor"

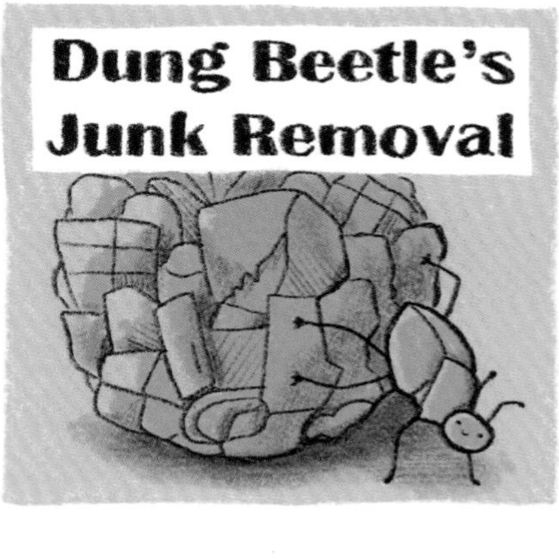

Dung Beetle's Junk Removal

Chapter 3: Knight School

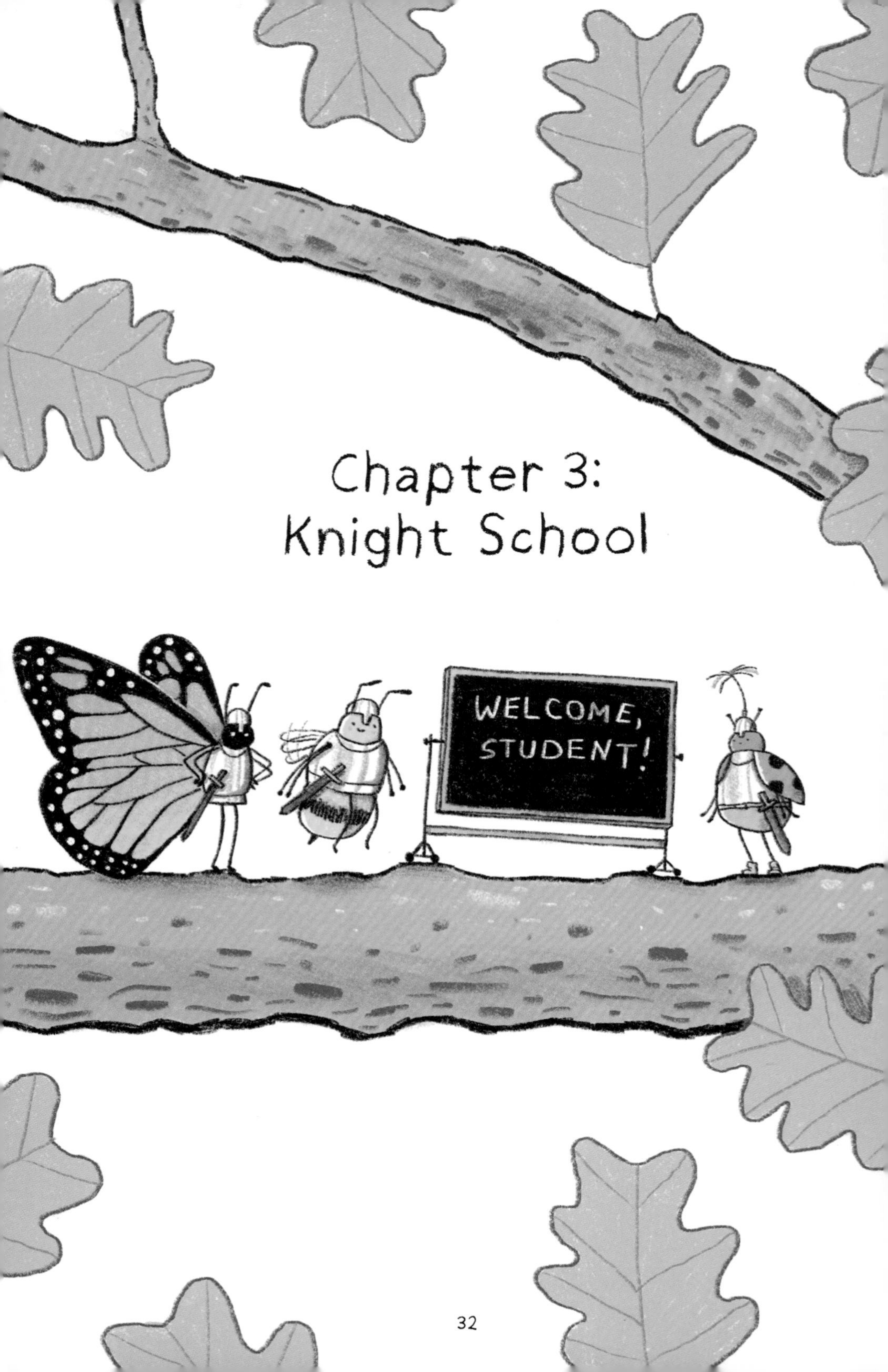
WELCOME, STUDENT!

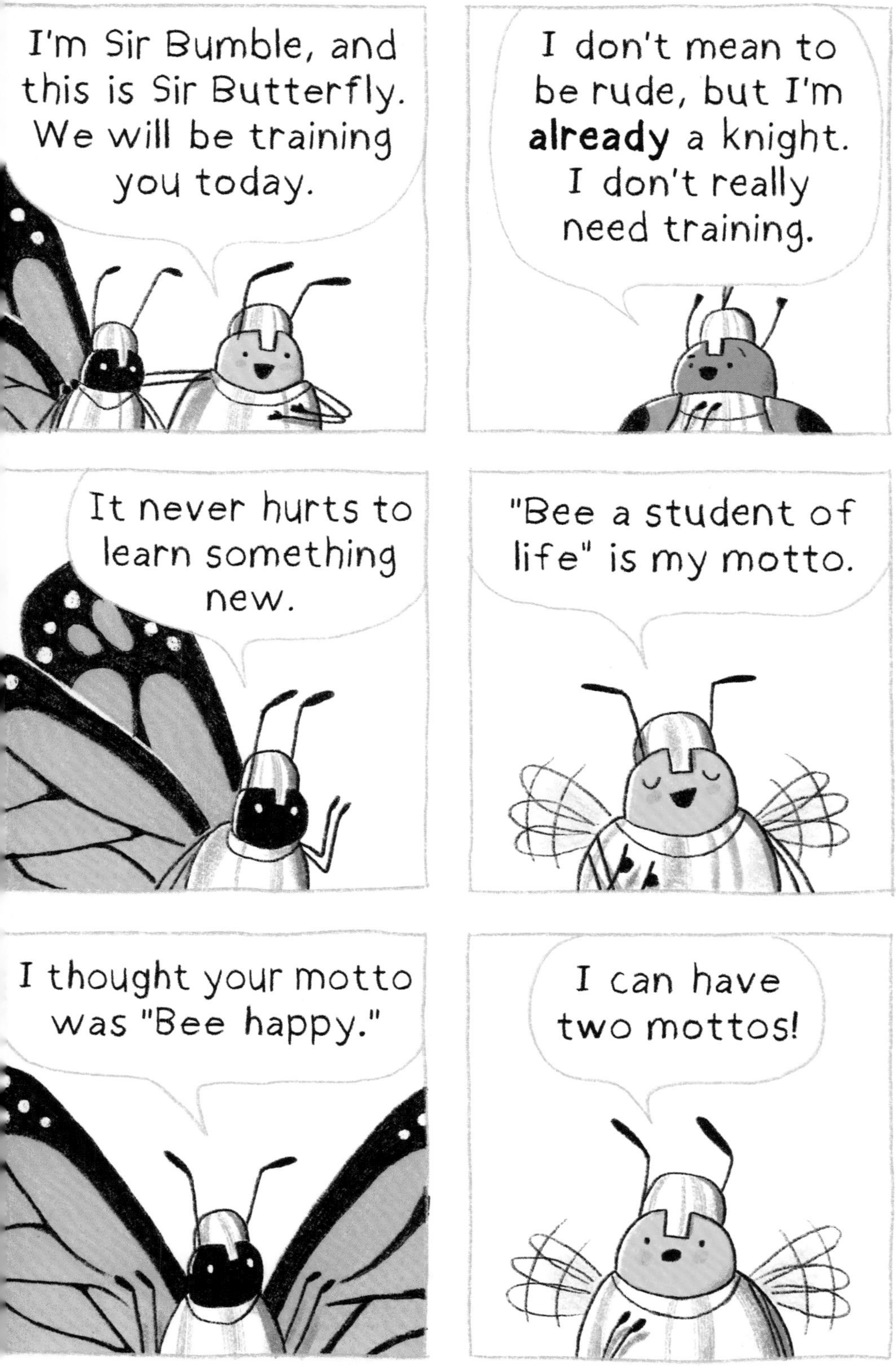
I'm Sir Bumble, and this is Sir Butterfly. We will be training you today.
I don't mean to be rude, but I'm **already** a knight. I don't really need training.
It never hurts to learn something new.
"Bee a student of life" is my motto.
I thought your motto was "Bee happy."
I can have two mottos!

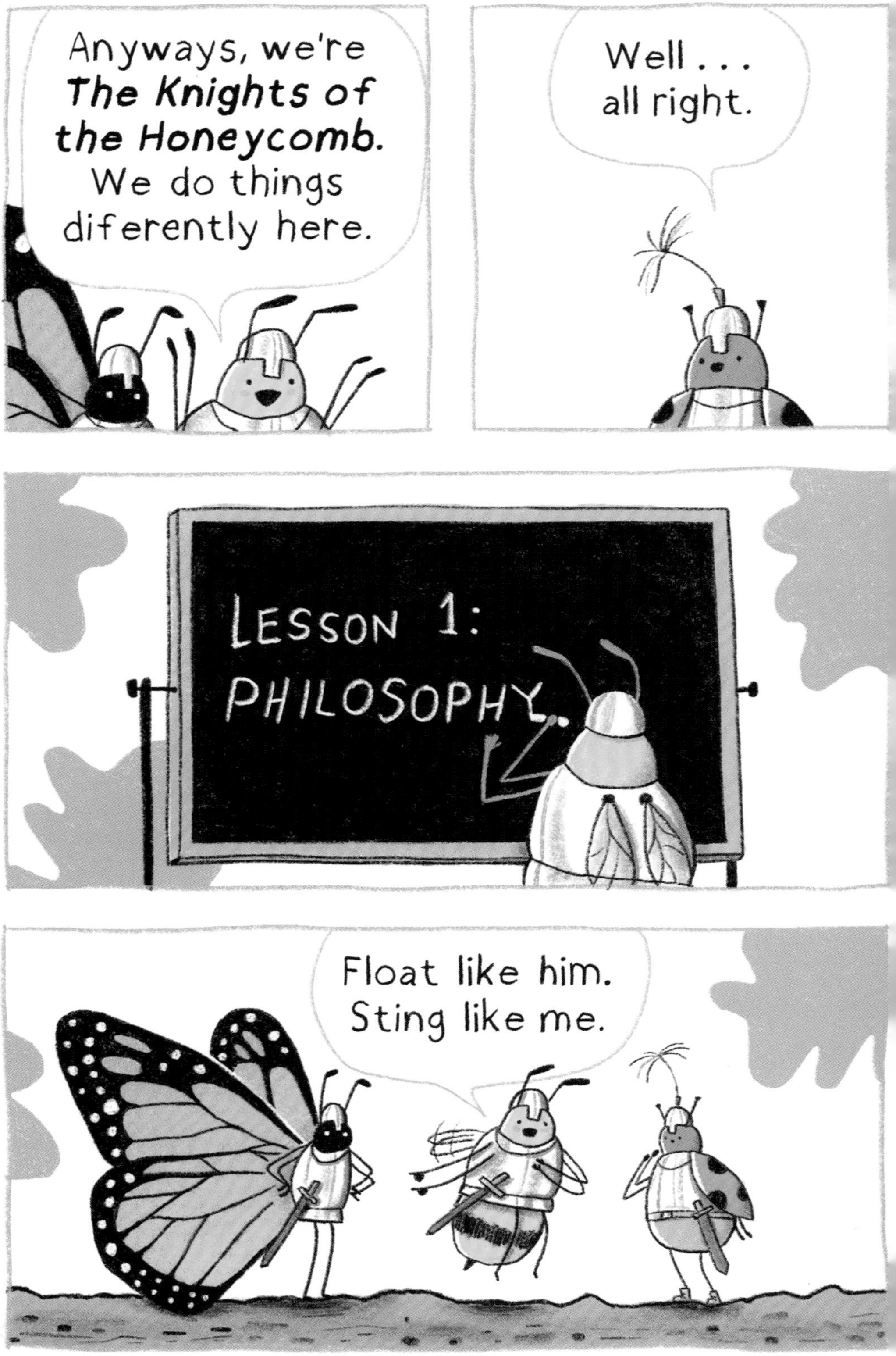
Anyways, we're **The Knights of the Honeycomb.** We do things diferently here.
Well . . . all right.
LESSON 1: PHILOSOPHY
Float like him. Sting like me.

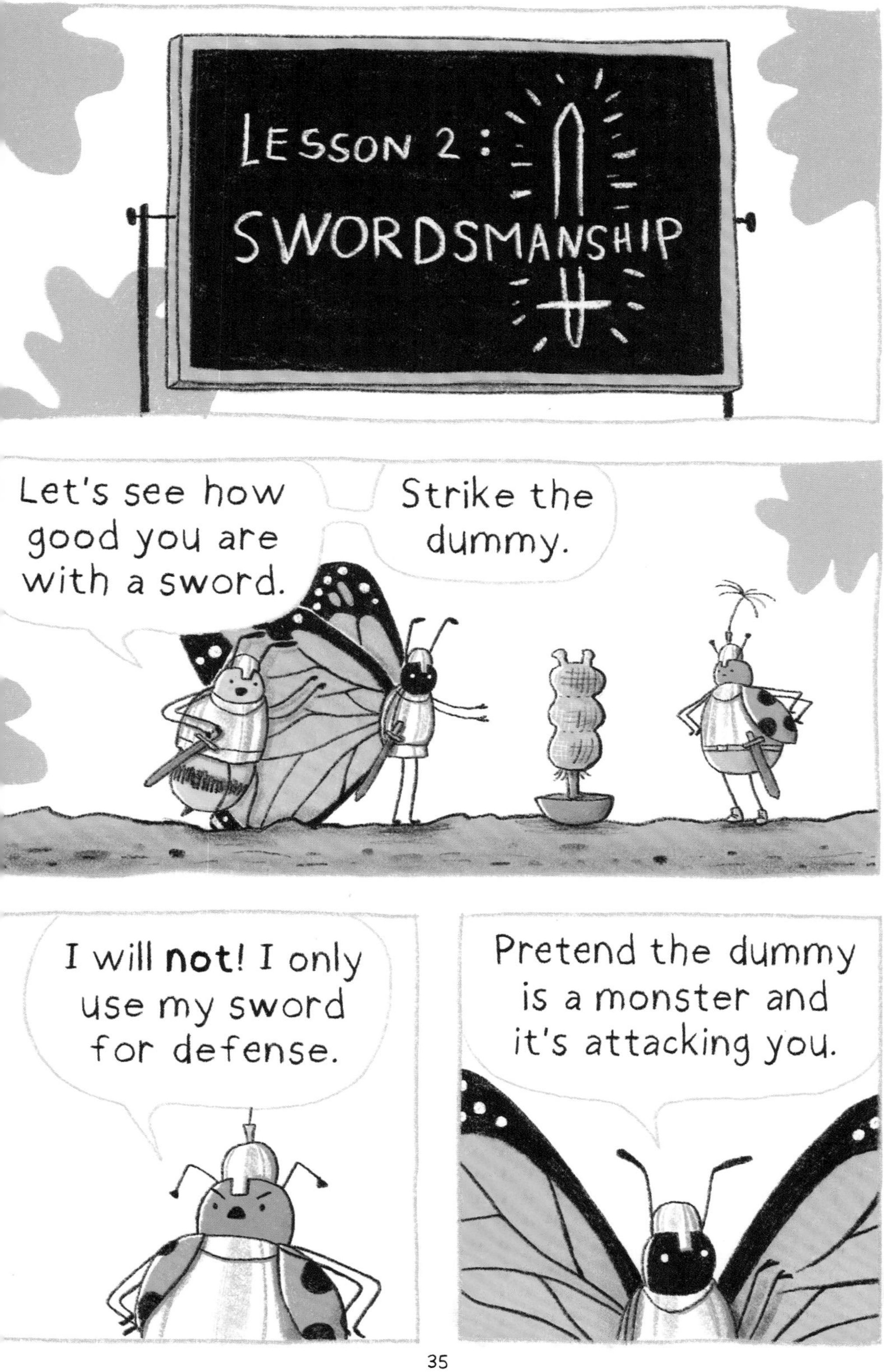
LESSON 2:
SWORDSMANSHIP
Let's see how good you are with a sword.
Strike the dummy.
I will **not**! I only use my sword for defense.
Pretend the dummy is a monster and it's attacking you.

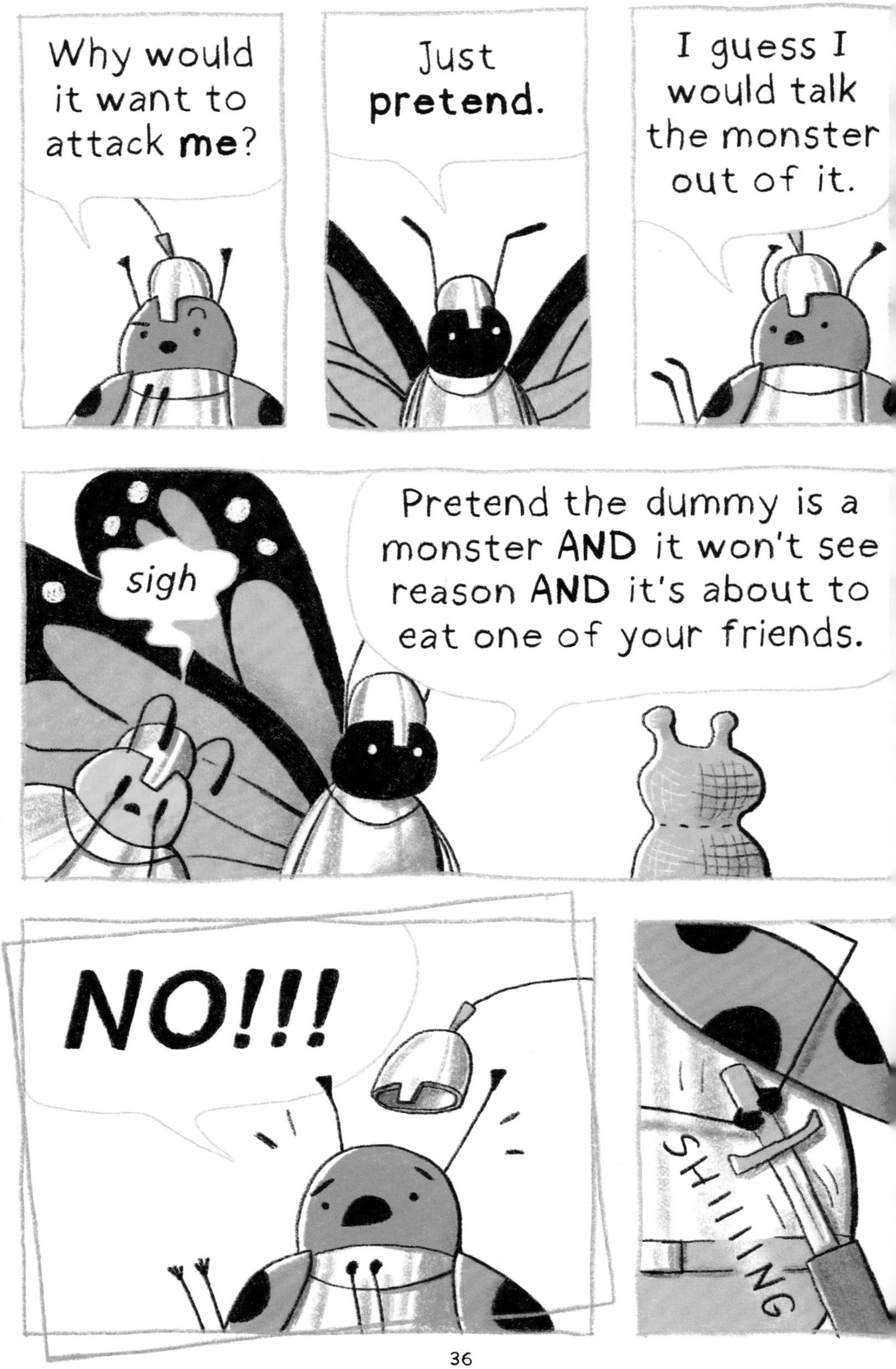
Why would it want to attack **me**?
Just **pretend**.
I guess I would talk the monster out of it.
sigh
Pretend the dummy is a monster **AND** it won't see reason **AND** it's about to eat one of your friends.
NO!!!
SHIIIING

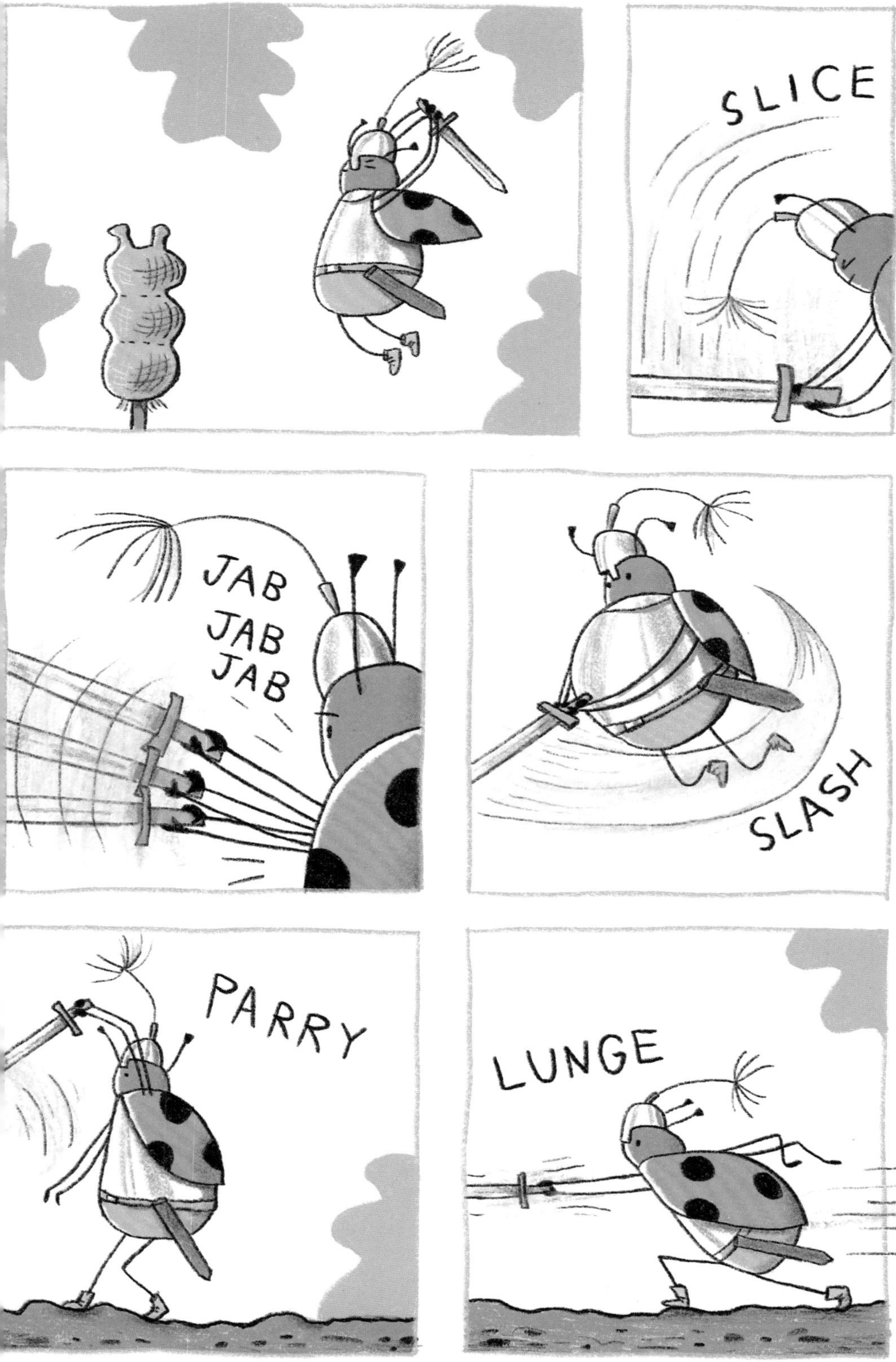
SLICE
JAB
JAB
JAB
SLASH
PARRY
LUNGE

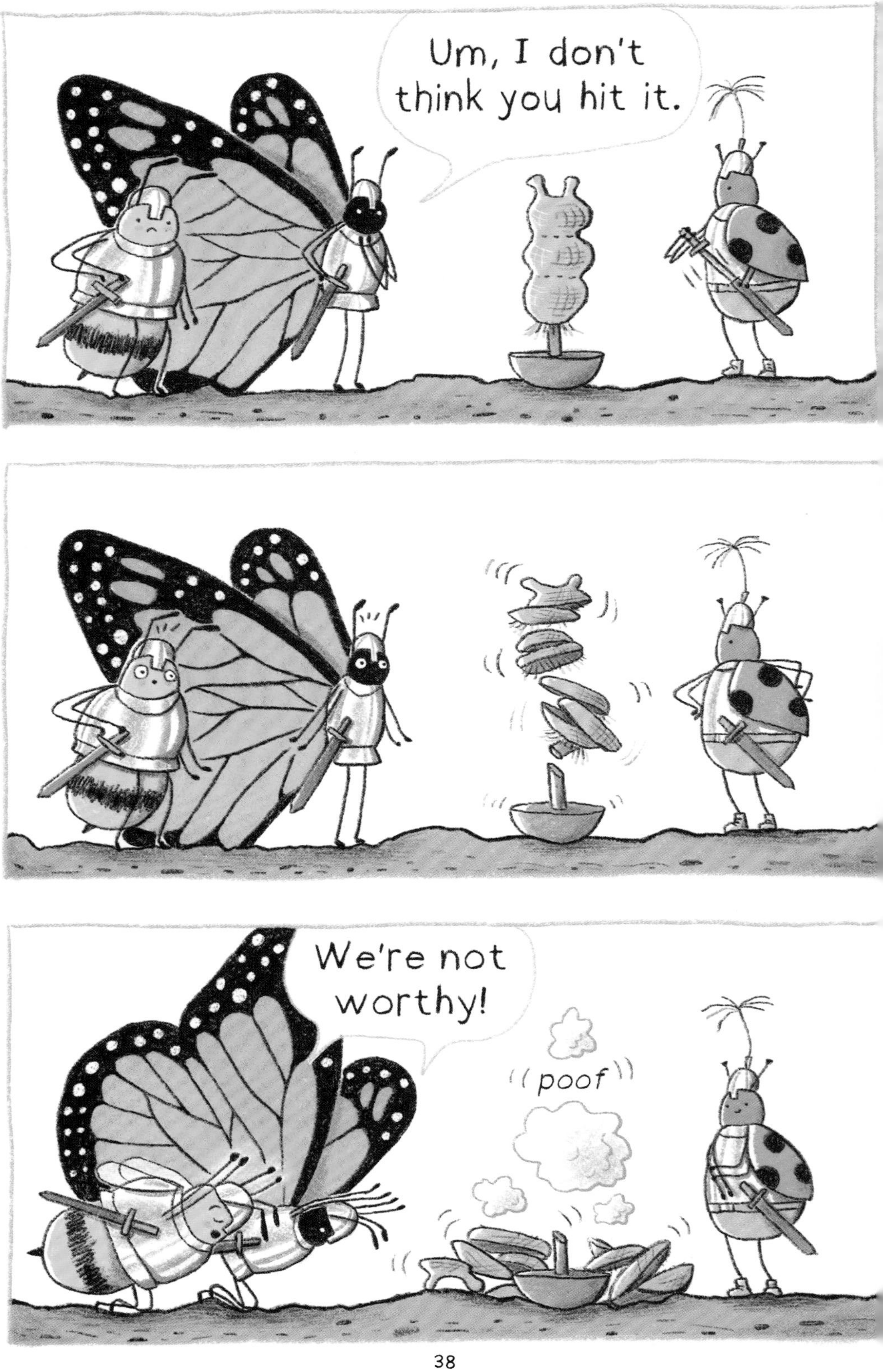
Um, I don't think you hit it.
We're not worthy!
poof

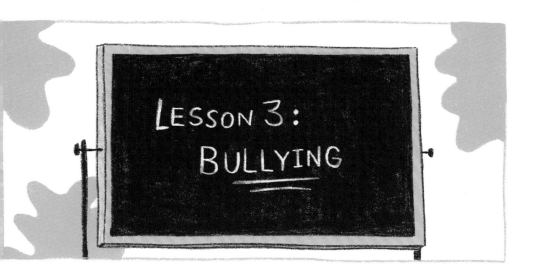

LESSON 3:
BULLYING

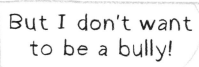

But I don't want to be a bully!

The queen was very clear. It's either this or jail.

Are you angry?

Yes.

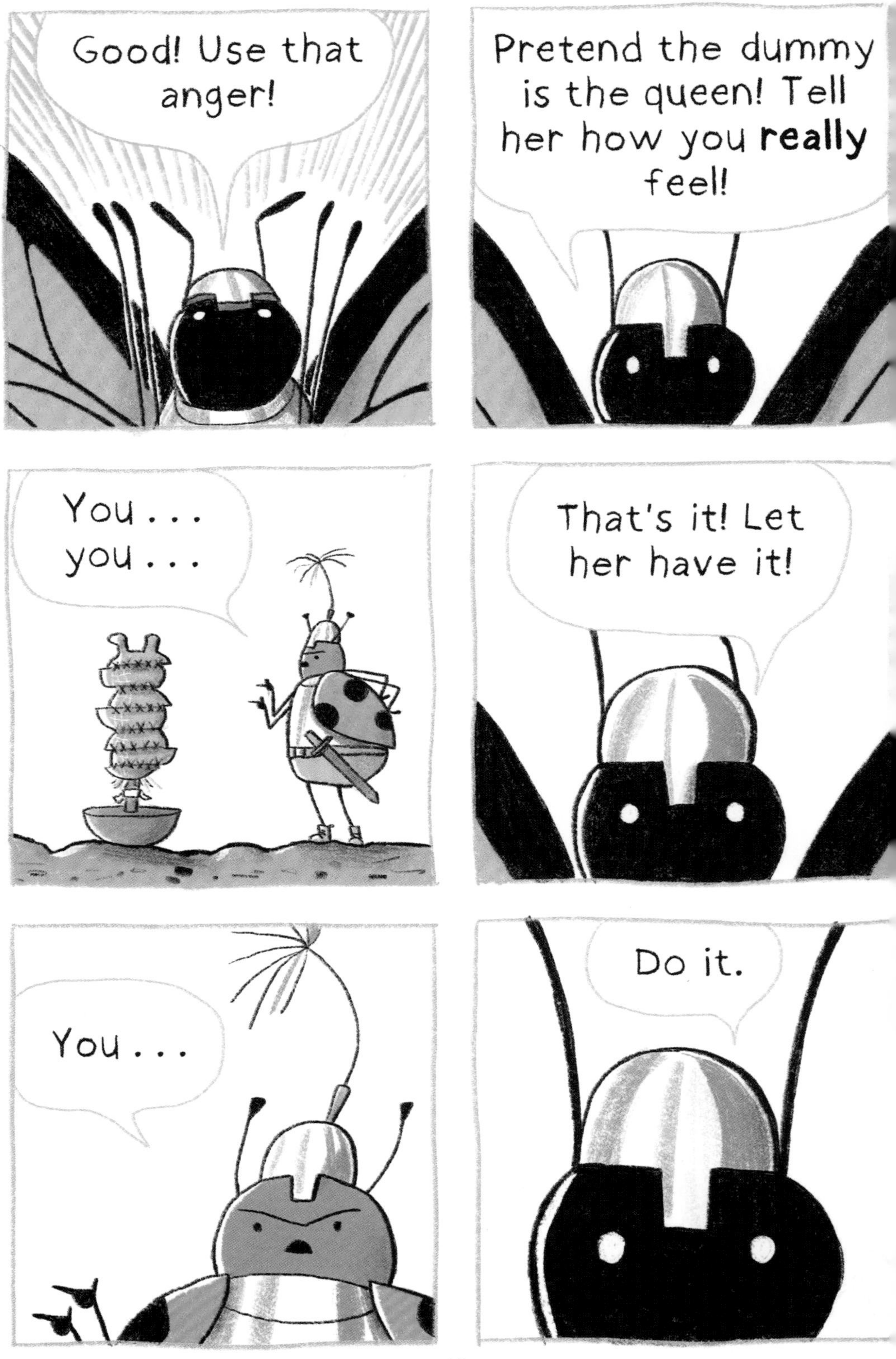
Good! Use that anger!
Pretend the dummy is the queen! Tell her how you **really** feel!
You . . . you . . .
That's it! Let her have it!
You . . .
Do it.

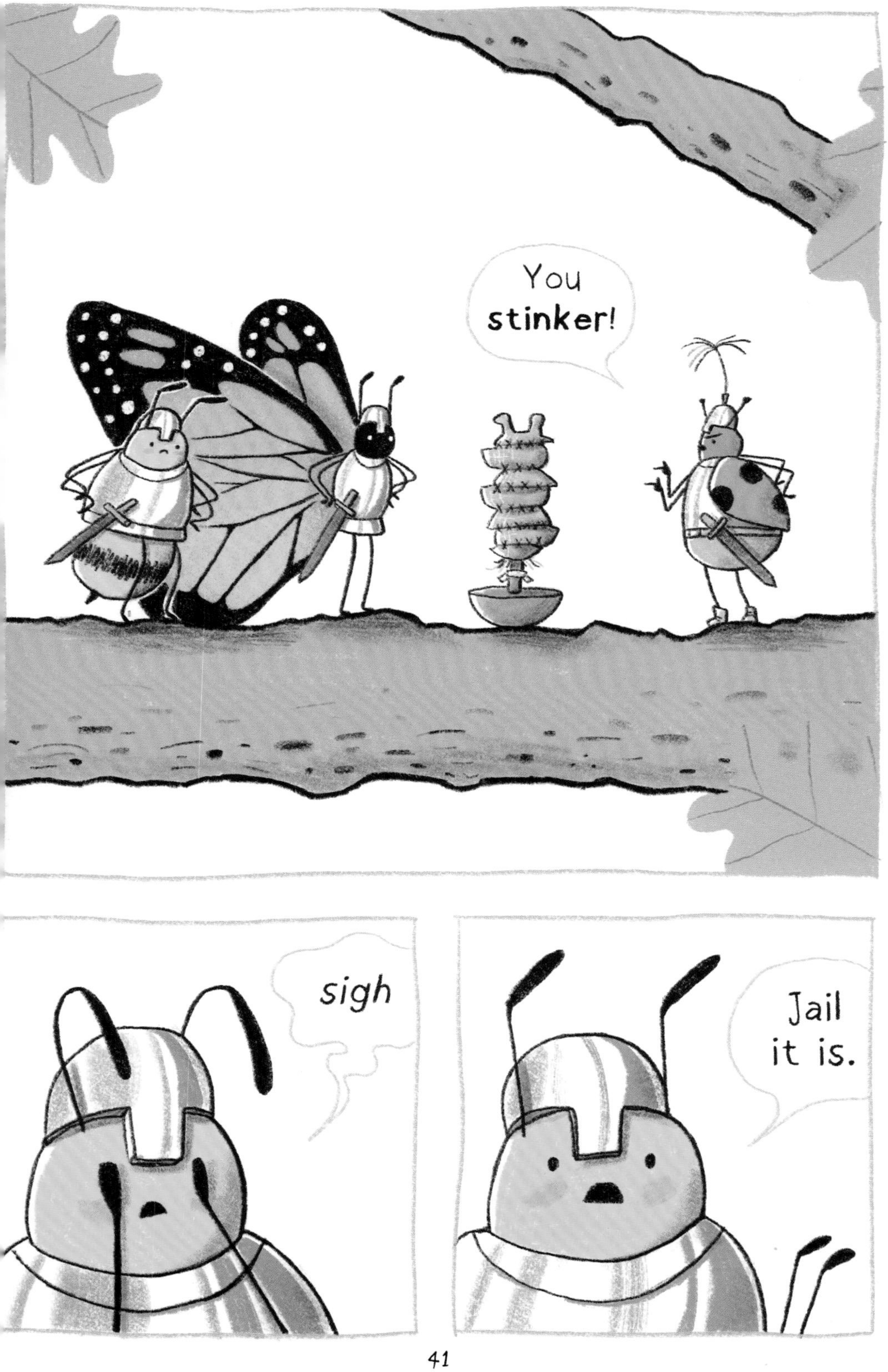
You **stinker!**
sigh
Jail it is.

Chapter 4: Jail

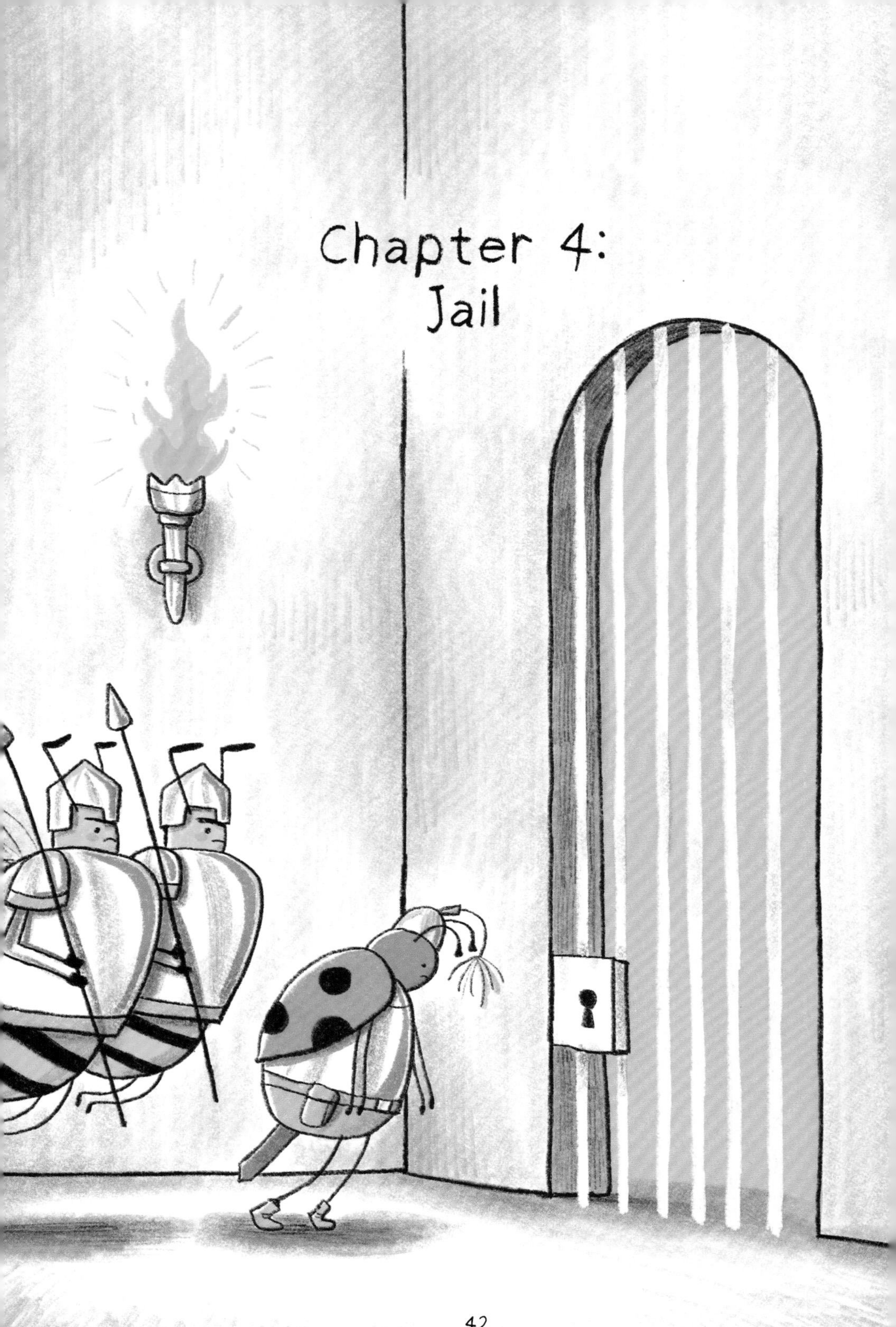

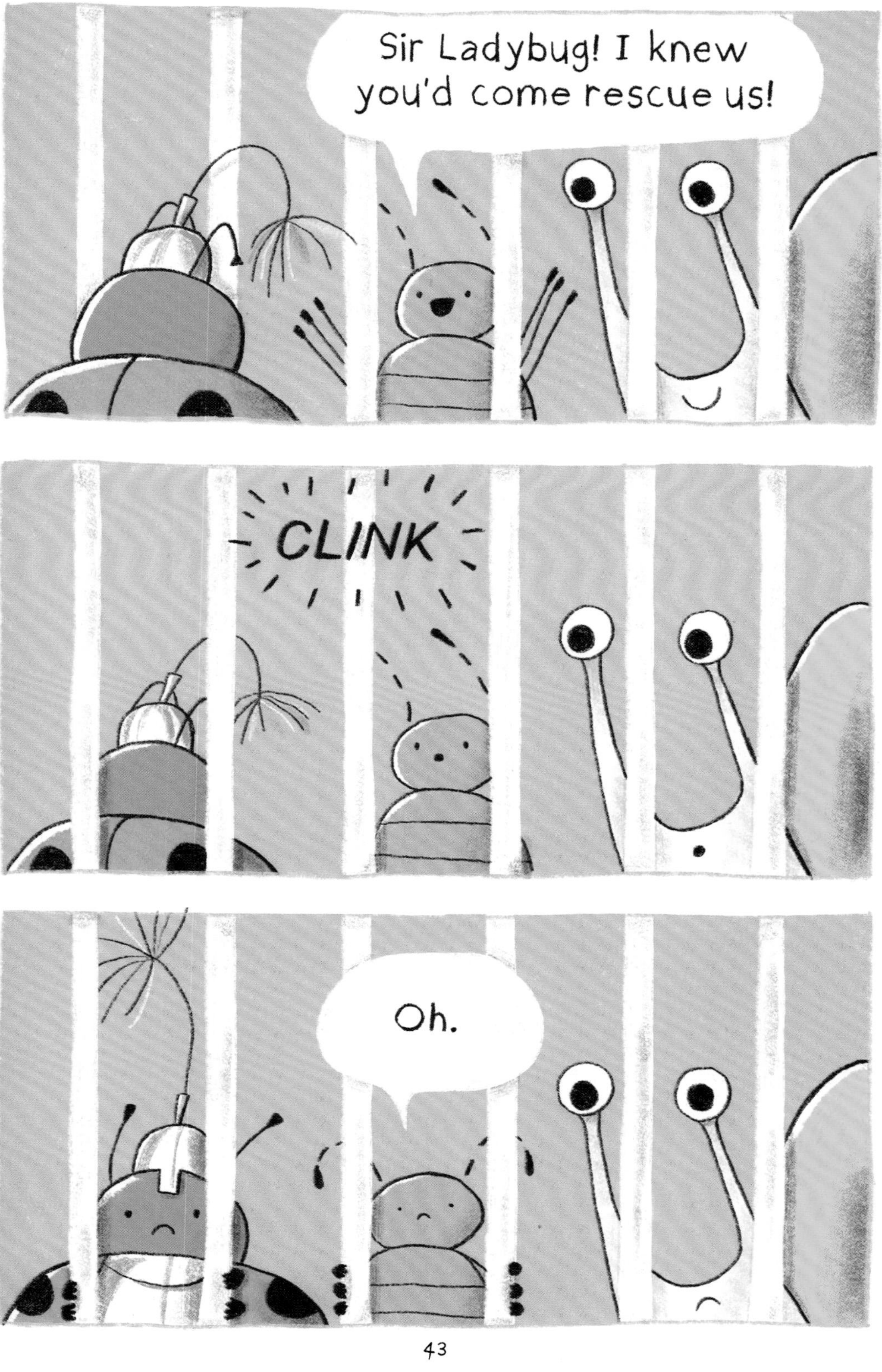
Sir Ladybug! I knew you'd come rescue us!
CLINK
Oh.

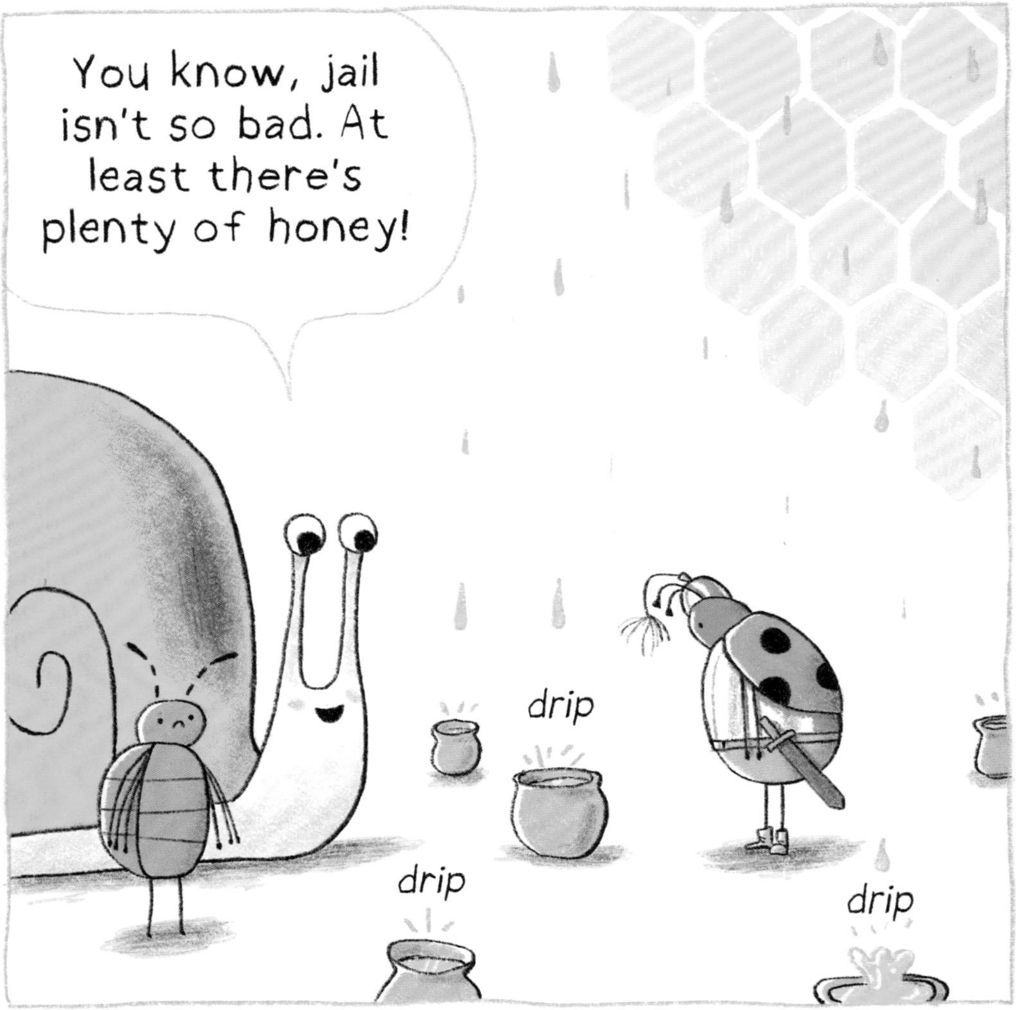
You know, jail isn't so bad. At least there's plenty of honey!
drip
drip
drip

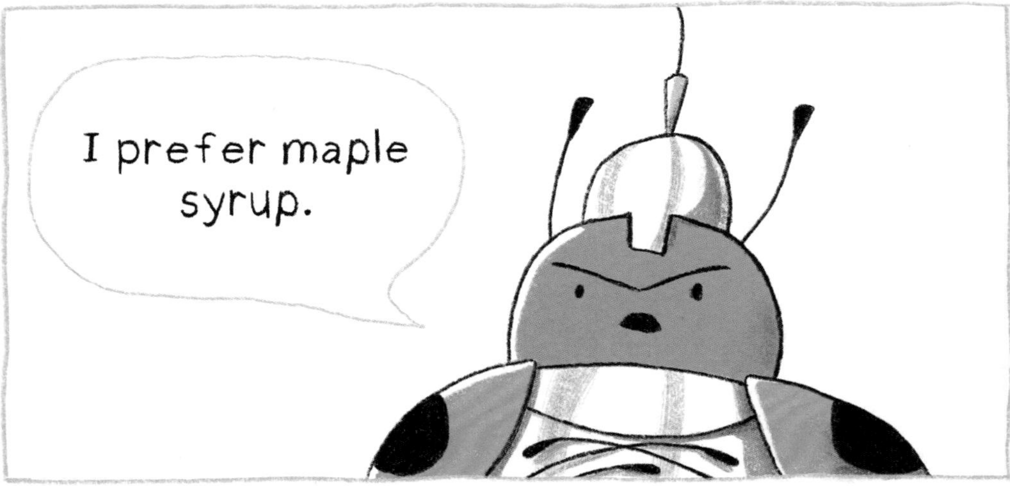
I prefer maple syrup.

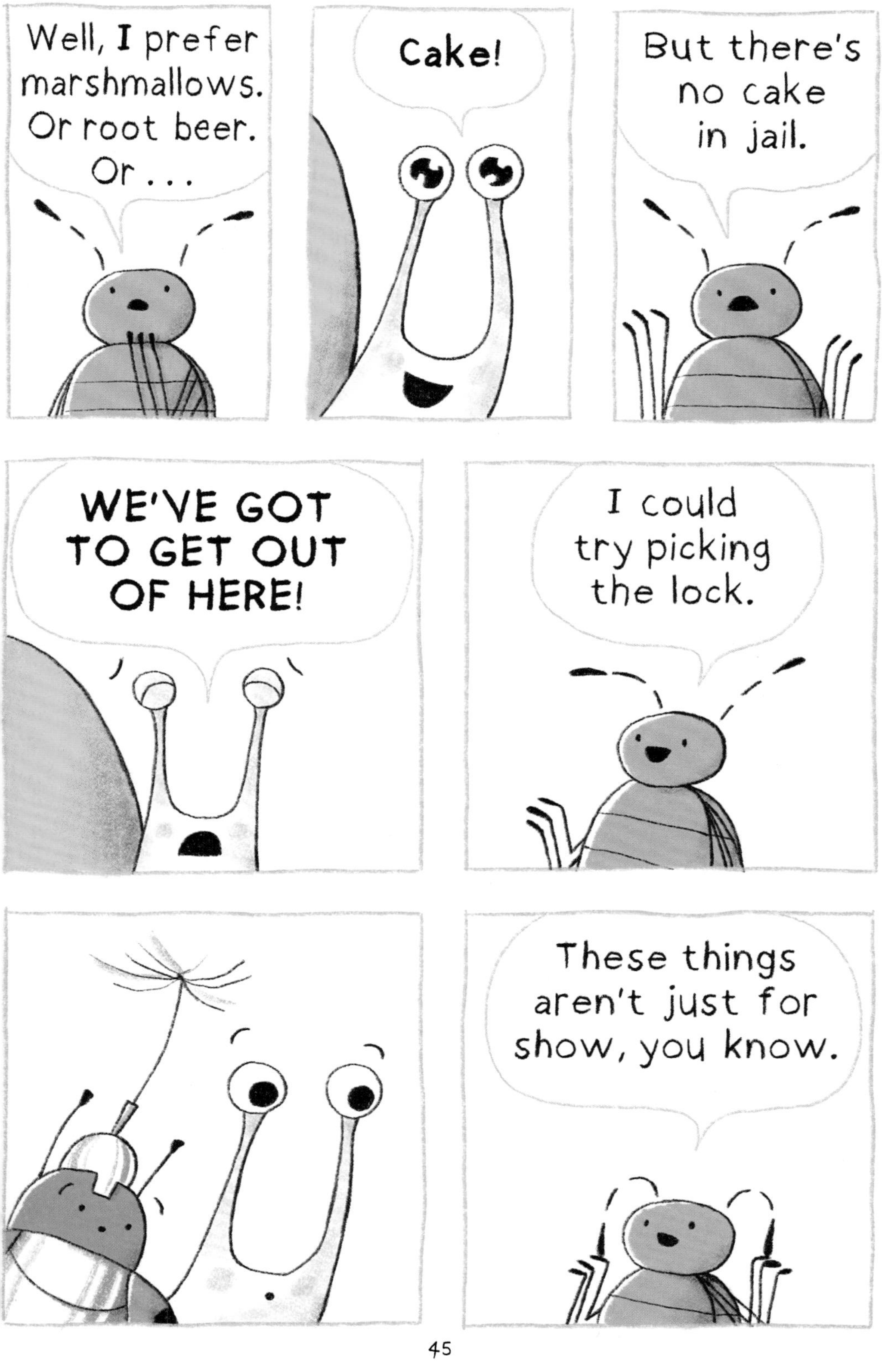
Well, **I** prefer marshmallows. Or root beer. Or . . .
Cake!
But there's no cake in jail.
WE'VE GOT TO GET OUT OF HERE!
I could try picking the lock.
These things aren't just for show, you know.

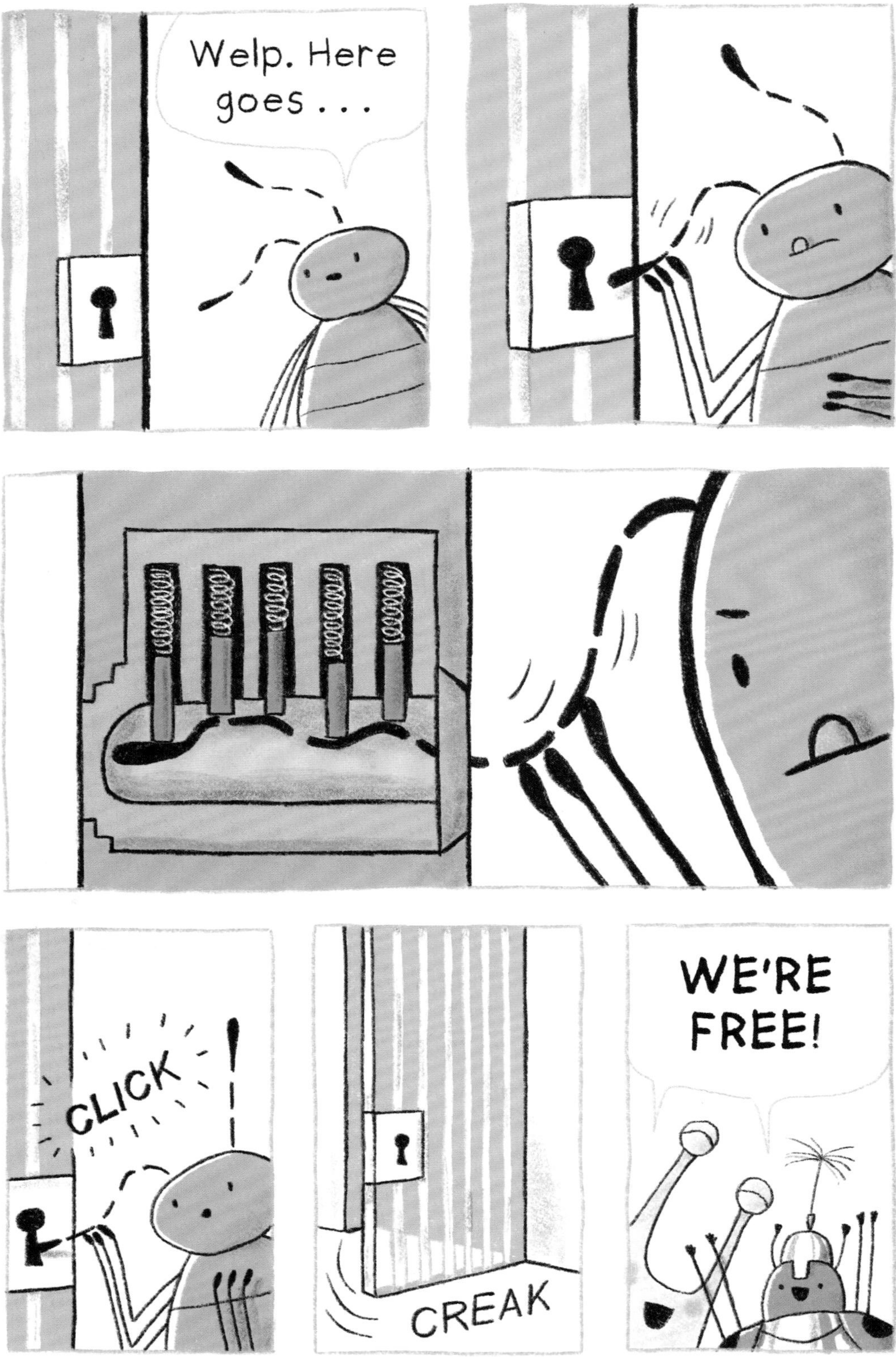
Welp. Here goes . . .
CLICK
CREAK
WE'RE FREE!

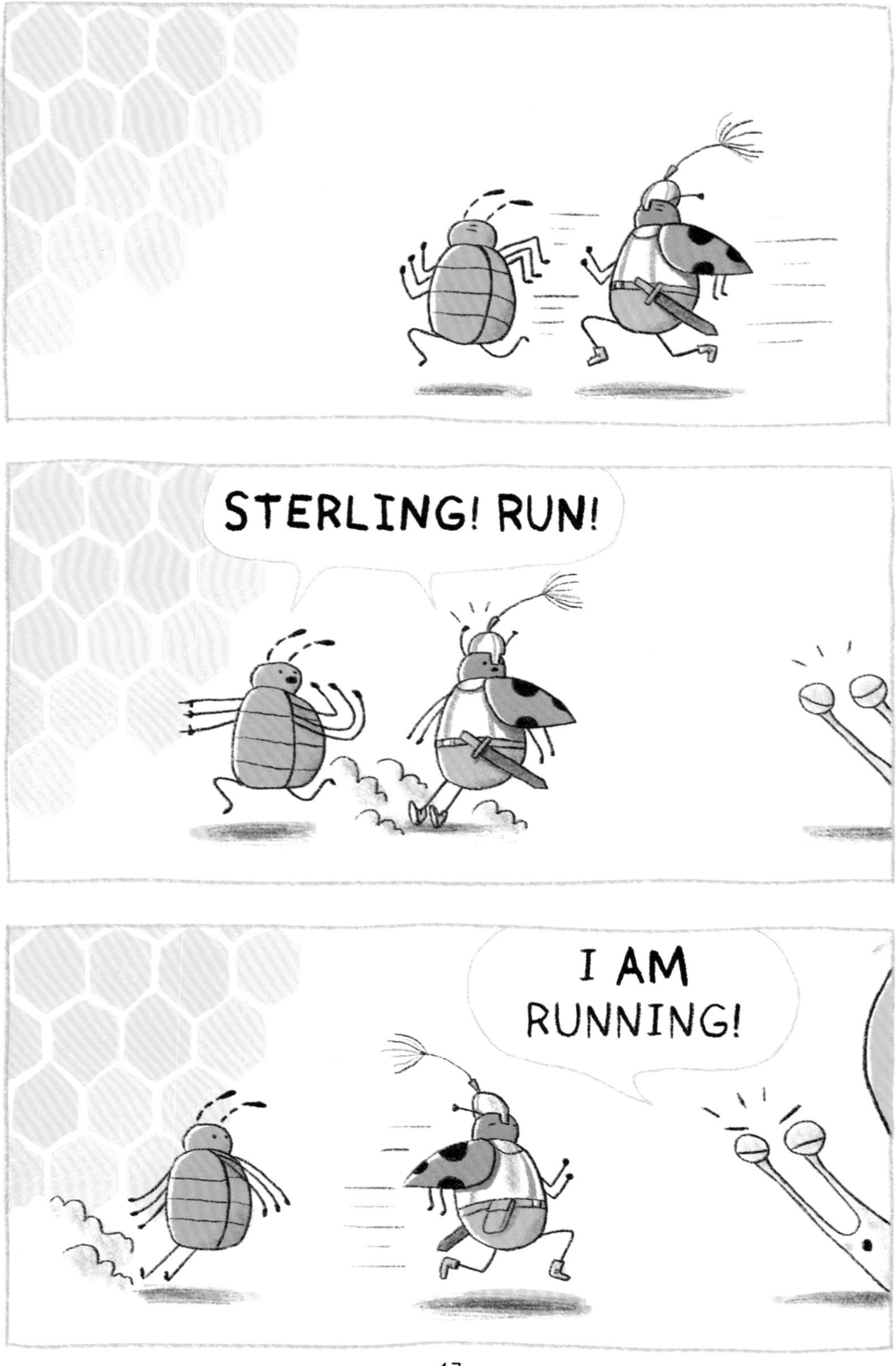
STERLING! RUN!
I AM RUNNING!

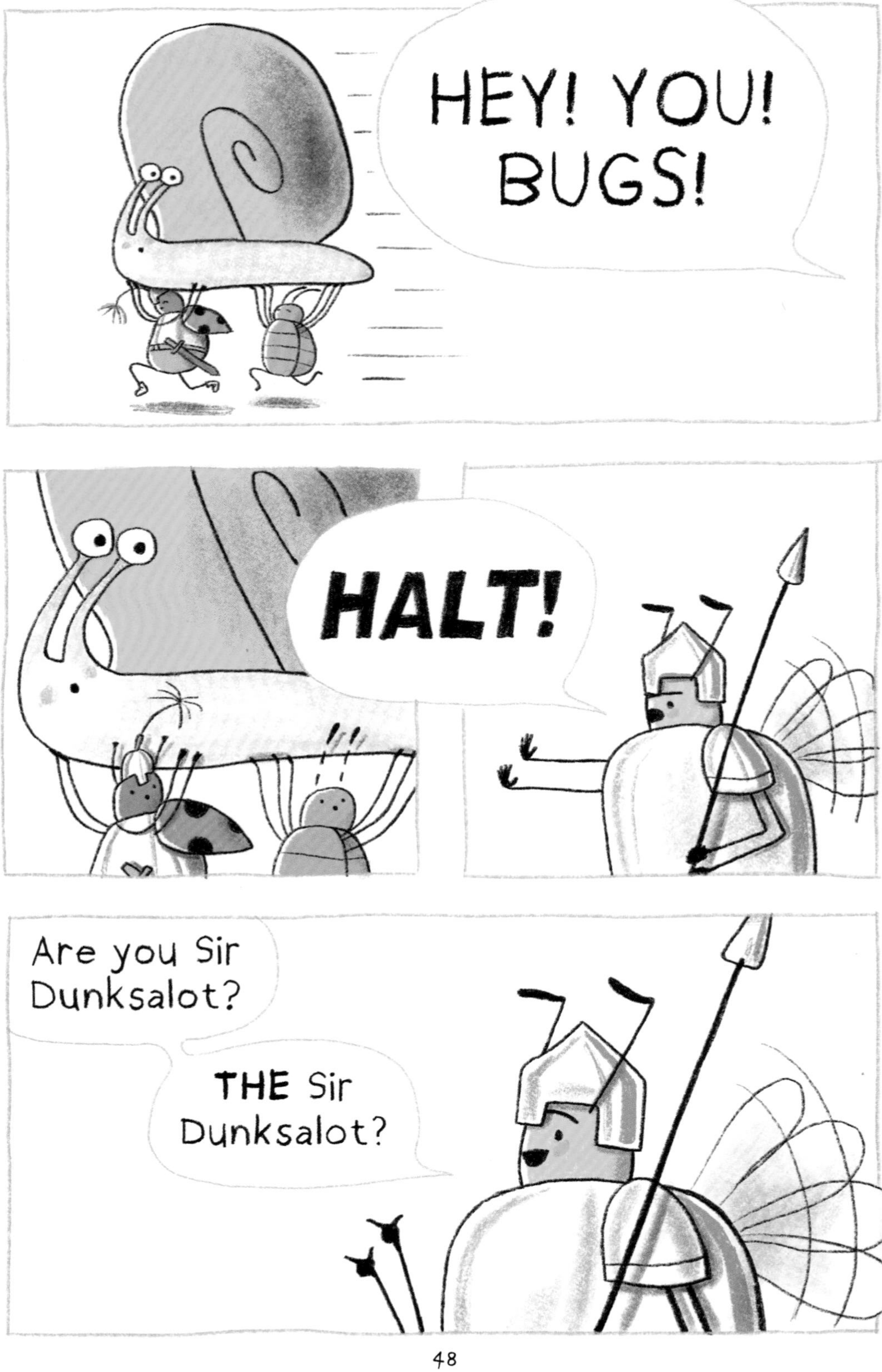
HEY! YOU! BUGS!
HALT!
Are you Sir Dunksalot?
THE Sir Dunksalot?

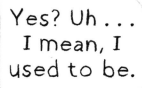

Yes? Uh . . . I mean, I used to be.

Are you going to arrest us?

Arrest you?

I'M YOUR BIGGEST FAN!

SIR DUNKSALOT!

So, you're going to let us go?

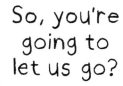

Of course! But first, can you just do one little thing for me . . . ?

Minutes later, in the queen's basketball court...

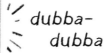

dubba-dubba

dubba-dubba

50

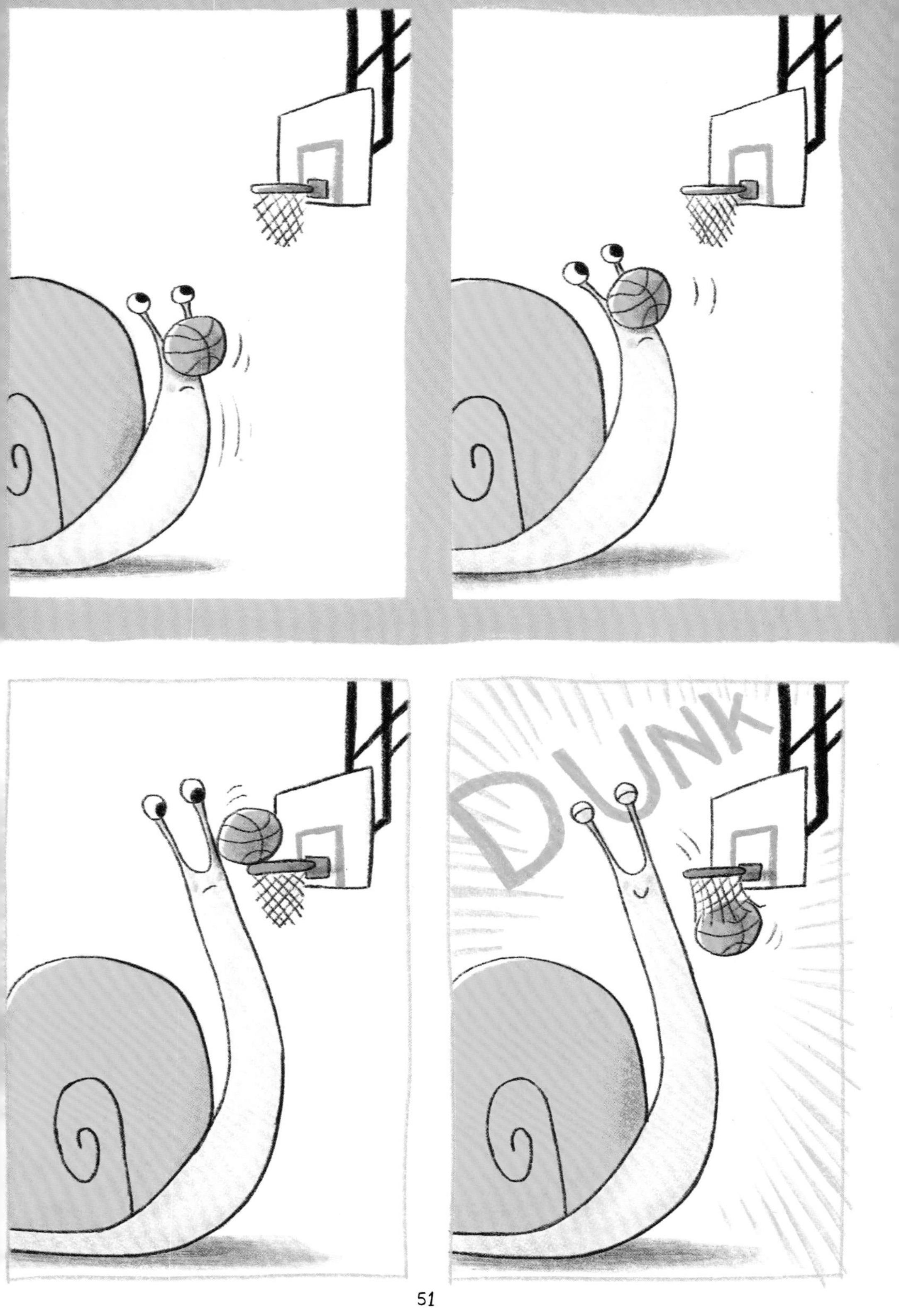
DUNK

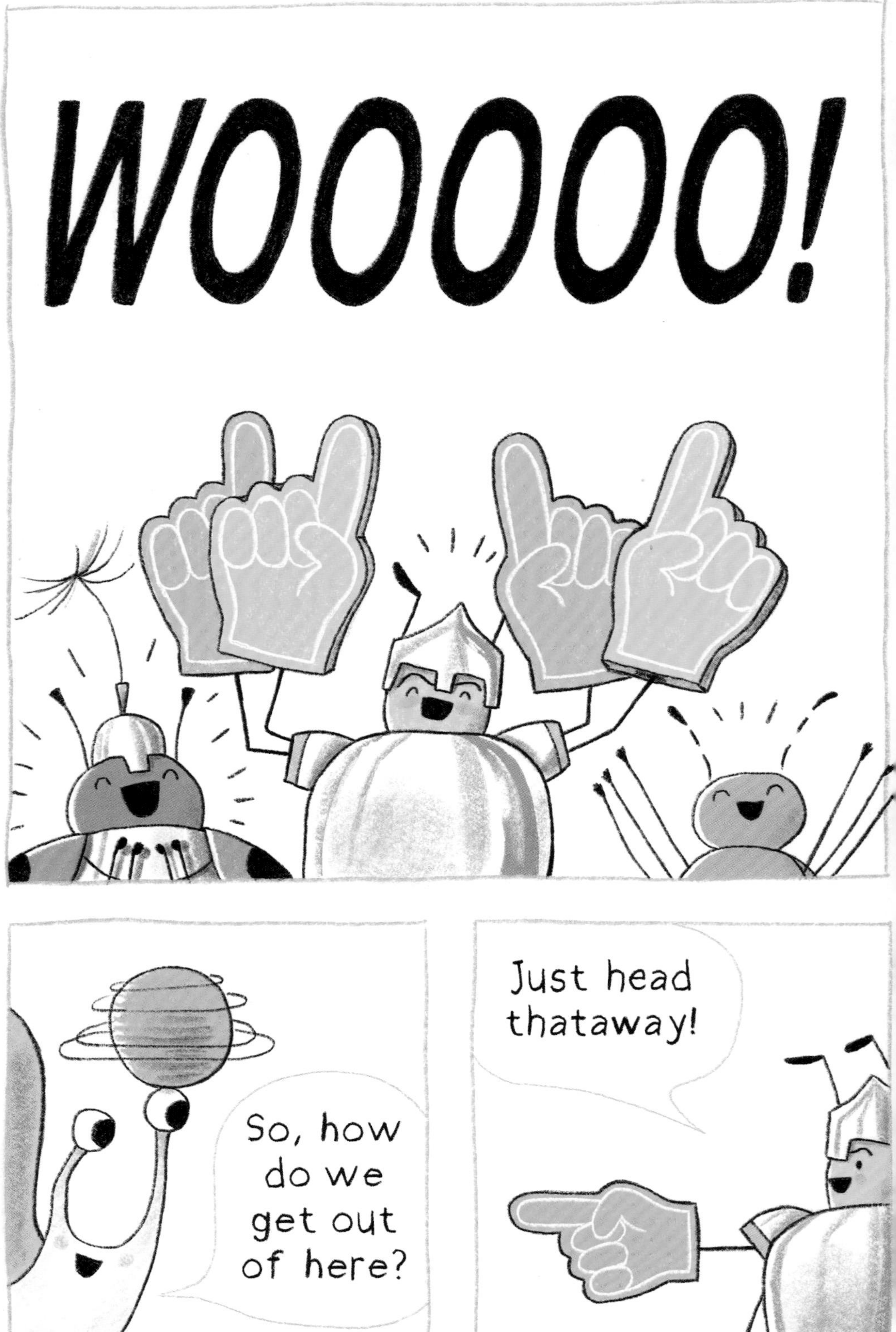
WOOOOO!
So, how do we get out of here?
Just head thataway!

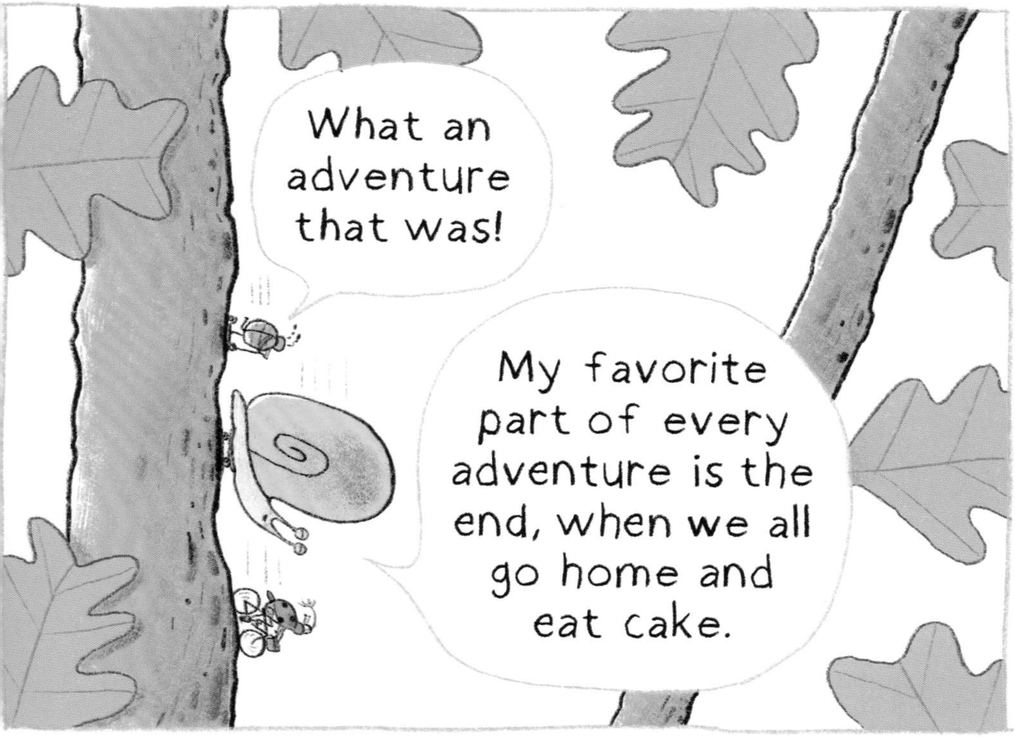
What an adventure that was!
My favorite part of every adventure is the end, when we all go home and eat cake.

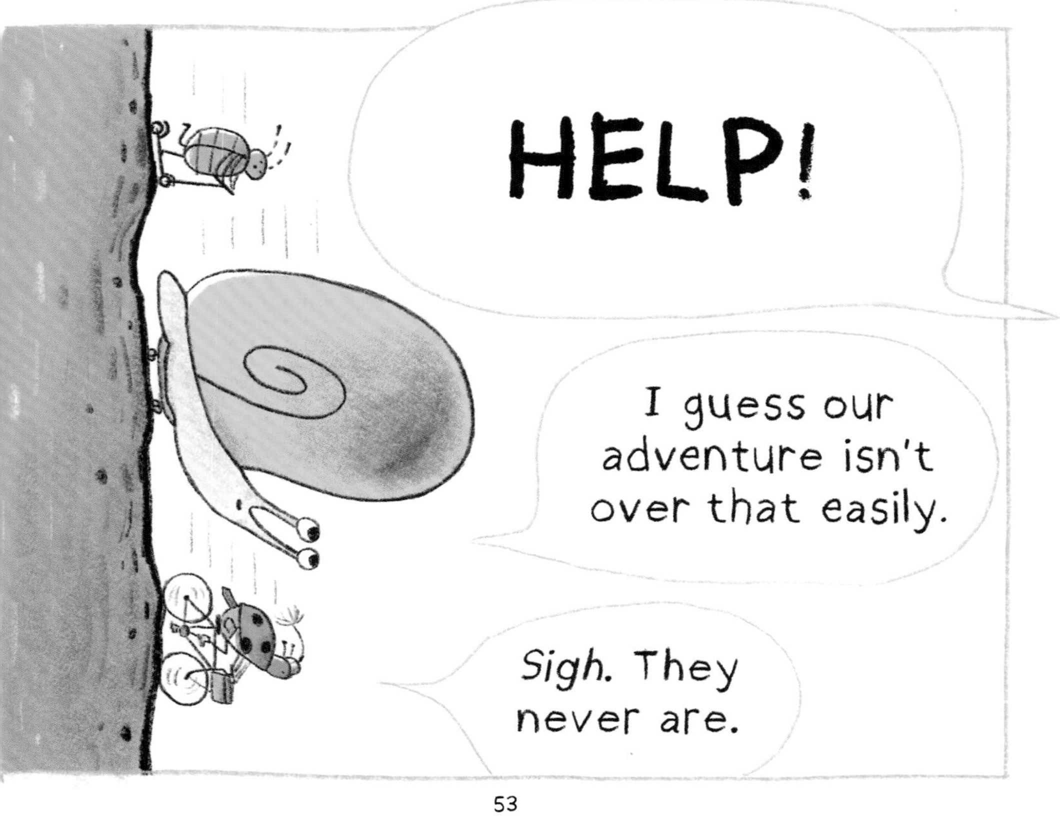
HELP!
I guess our adventure isn't over that easily.
Sigh. They never are.

Chapter 5: Trapped

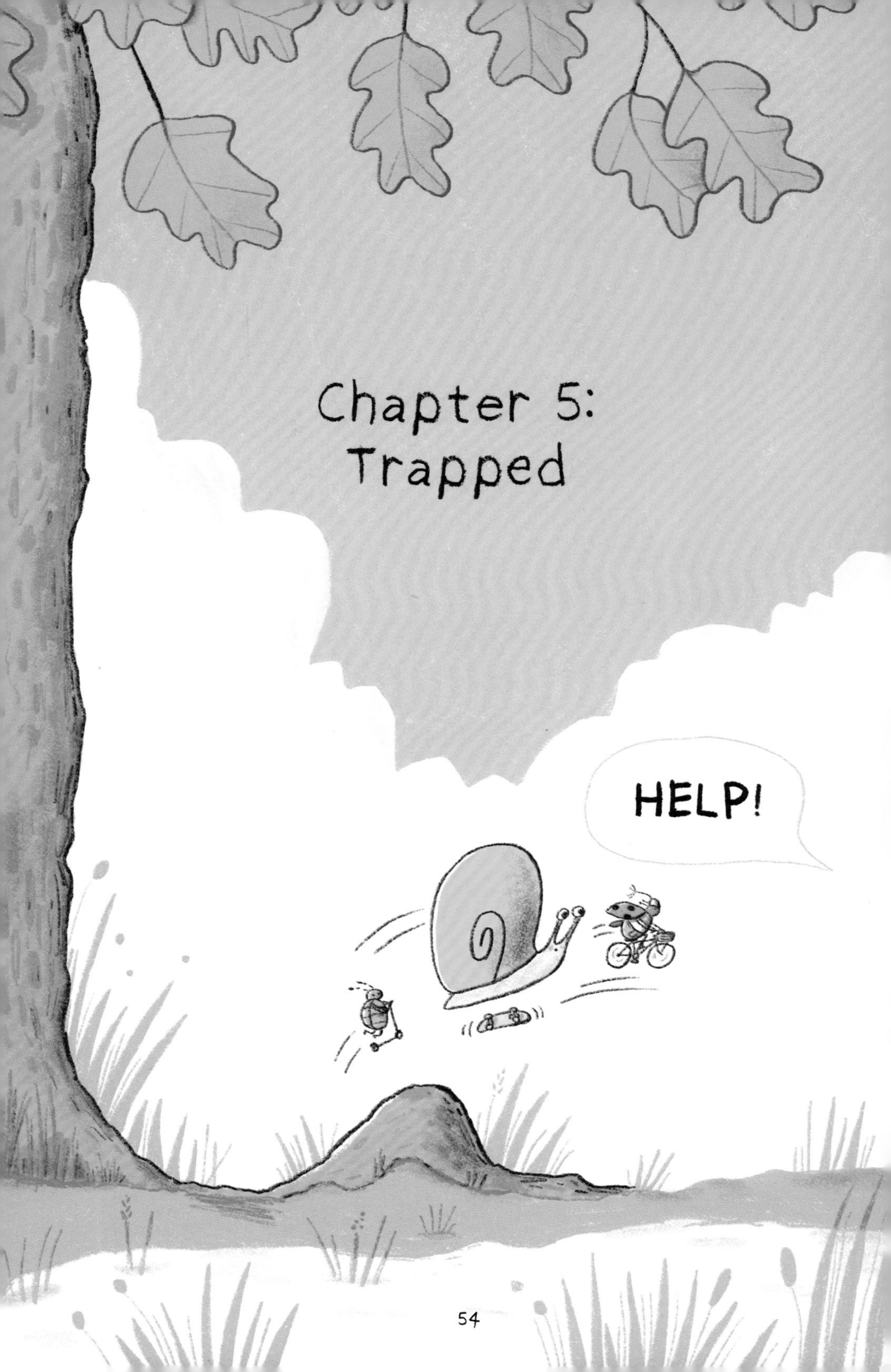
HELP!

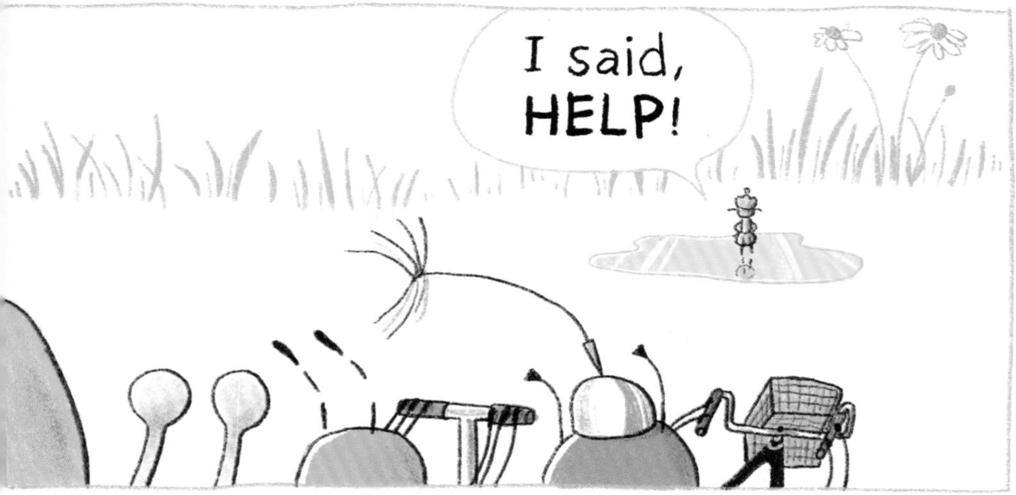
I said,
HELP!

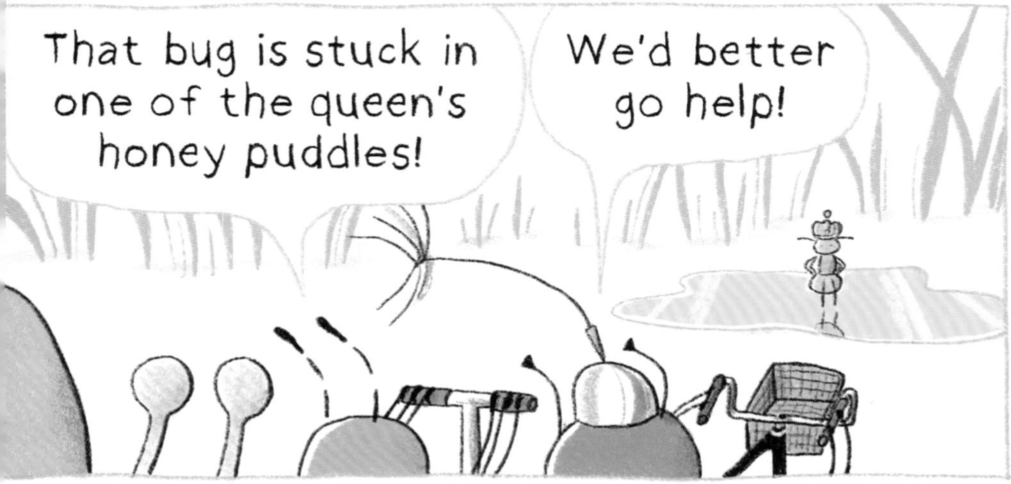
That bug is stuck in one of the queen's honey puddles!
We'd better go help!

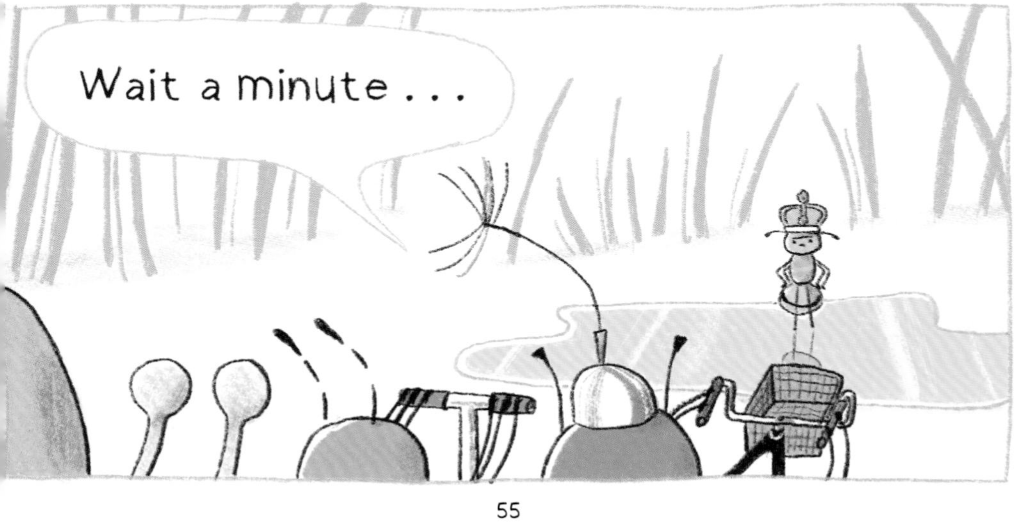
Wait a minute . . .

Um . . . Are you stuck?

How dare you ask me that! **I AM THE QUEEN!**

I'll take that as a yes.

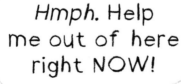

Hmph. Help me out of here right NOW!

Do we have to?

I think we do.

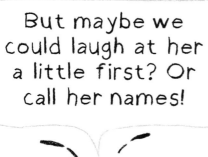
But maybe we could laugh at her a little first? Or call her names!

Pell . . .

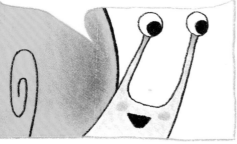
She **did** get stuck in her own trap. Can't we enjoy the irony*?

Sterling . . .

*irony: when a bee gets stuck in her own honey

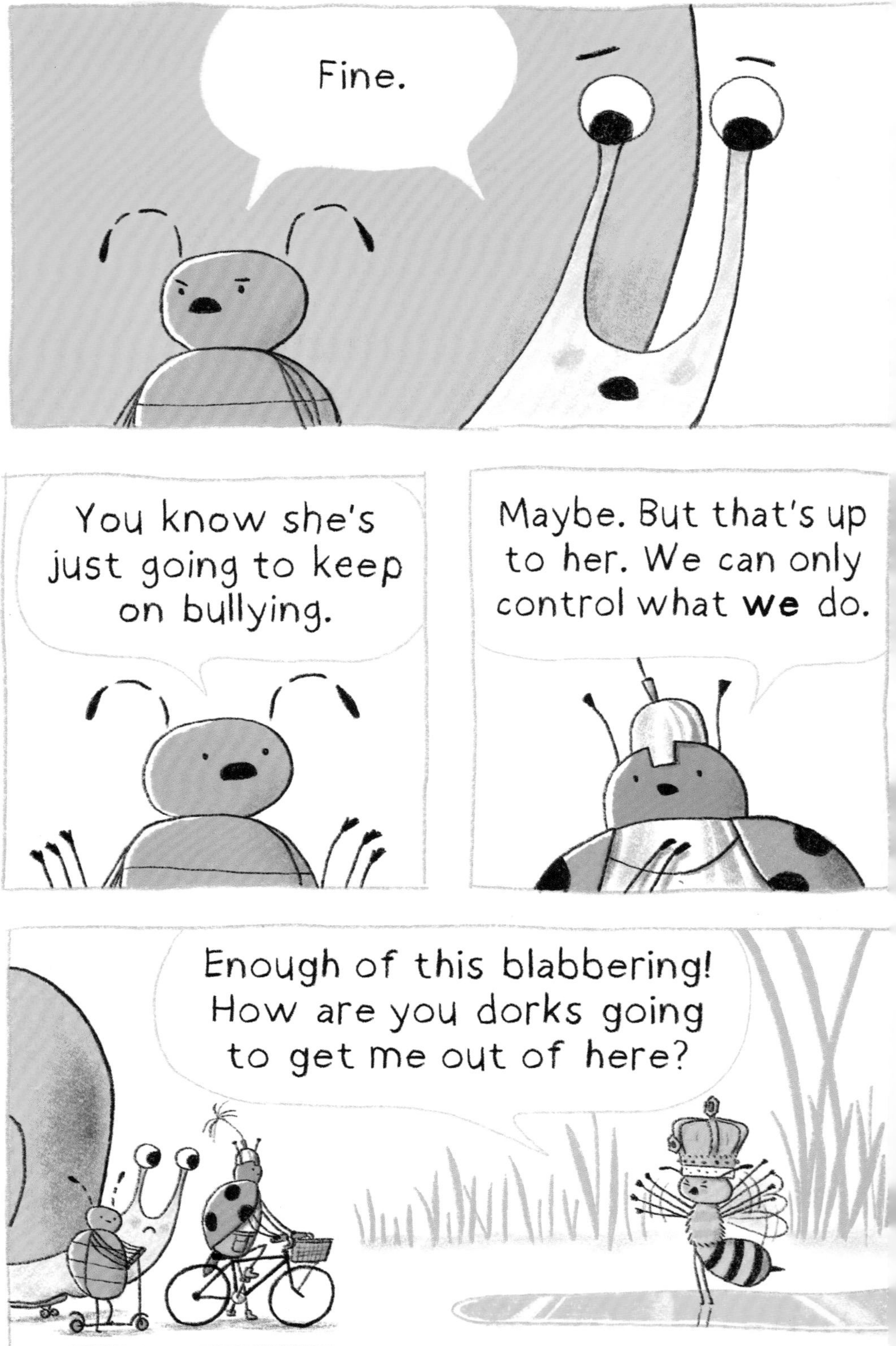
Fine.
You know she's just going to keep on bullying.
Maybe. But that's up to her. We can only control what **we** do.
Enough of this blabbering! How are you dorks going to get me out of here?

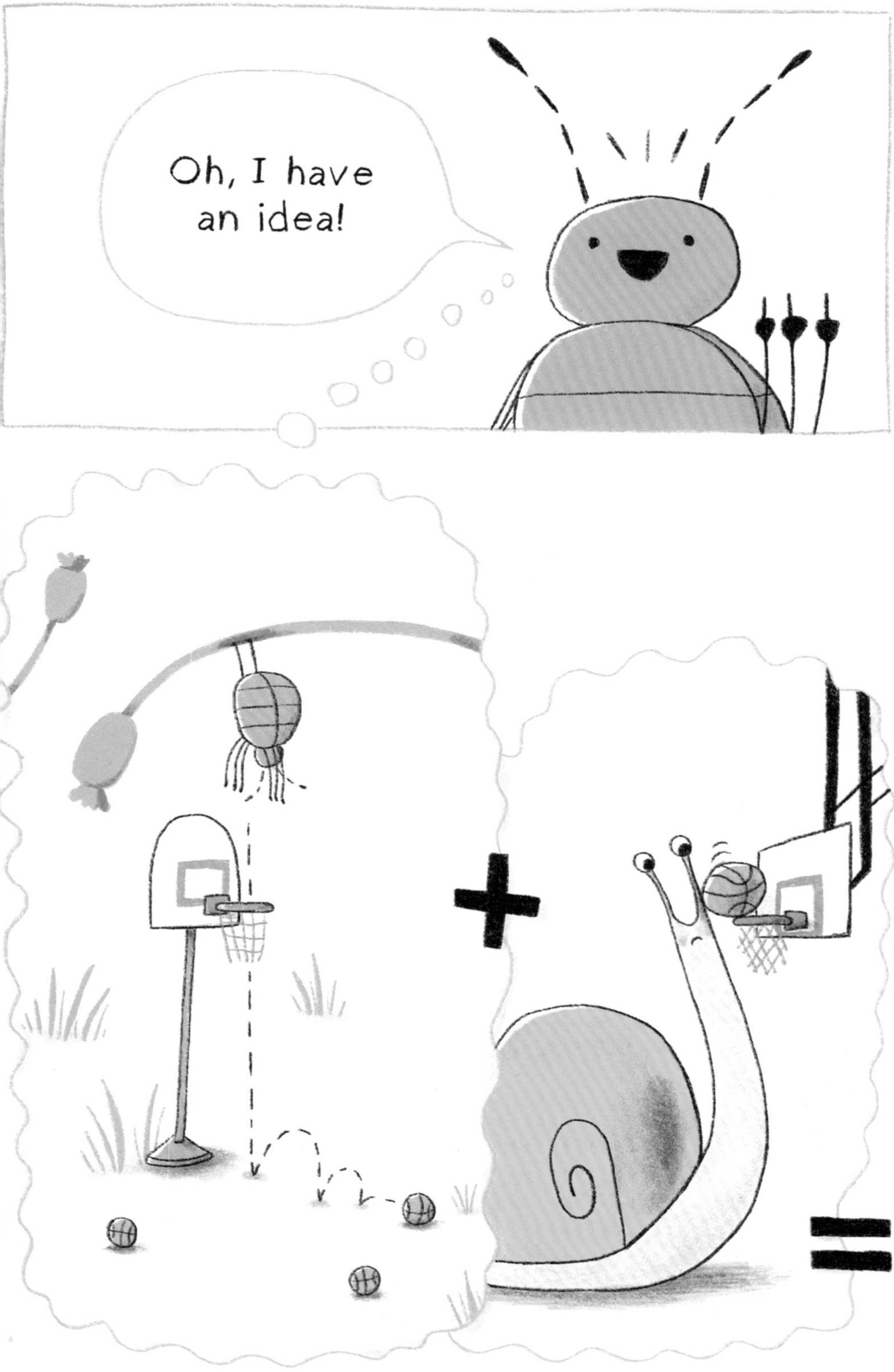
Oh, I have an idea!
+
=

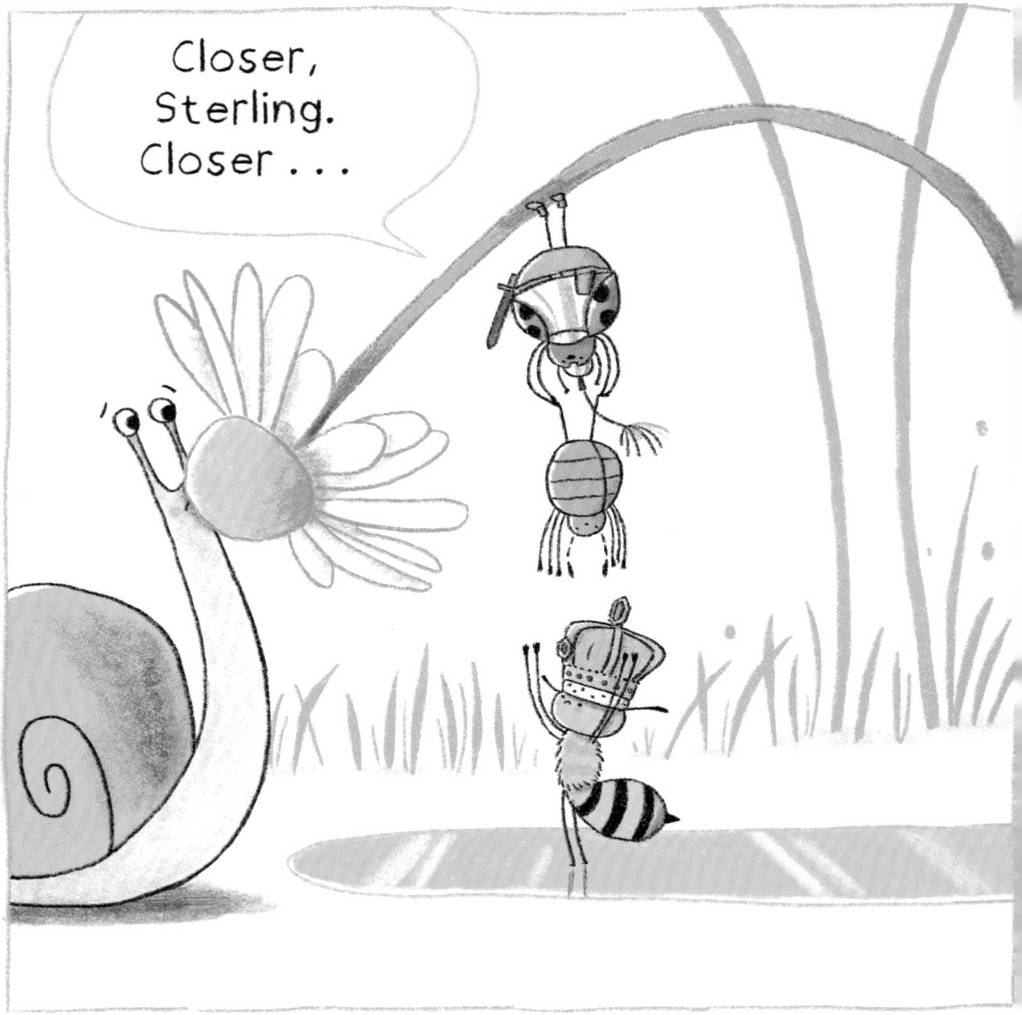
Closer,
Sterling.
Closer . . .

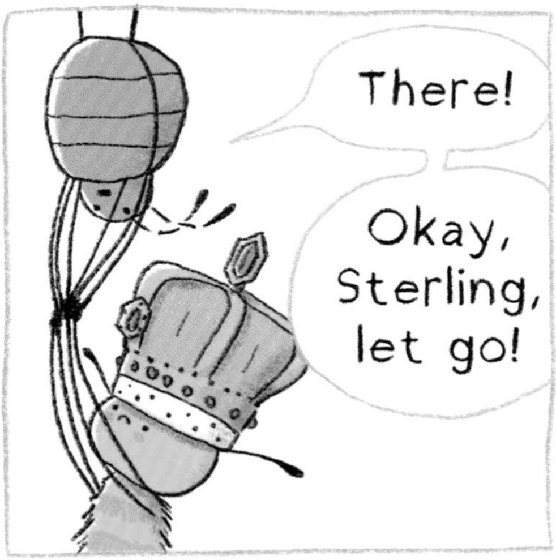
There!
Okay,
Sterling,
let go!

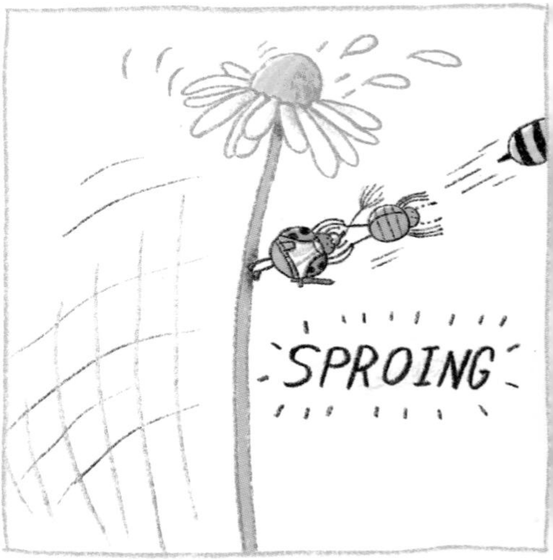
SPROING

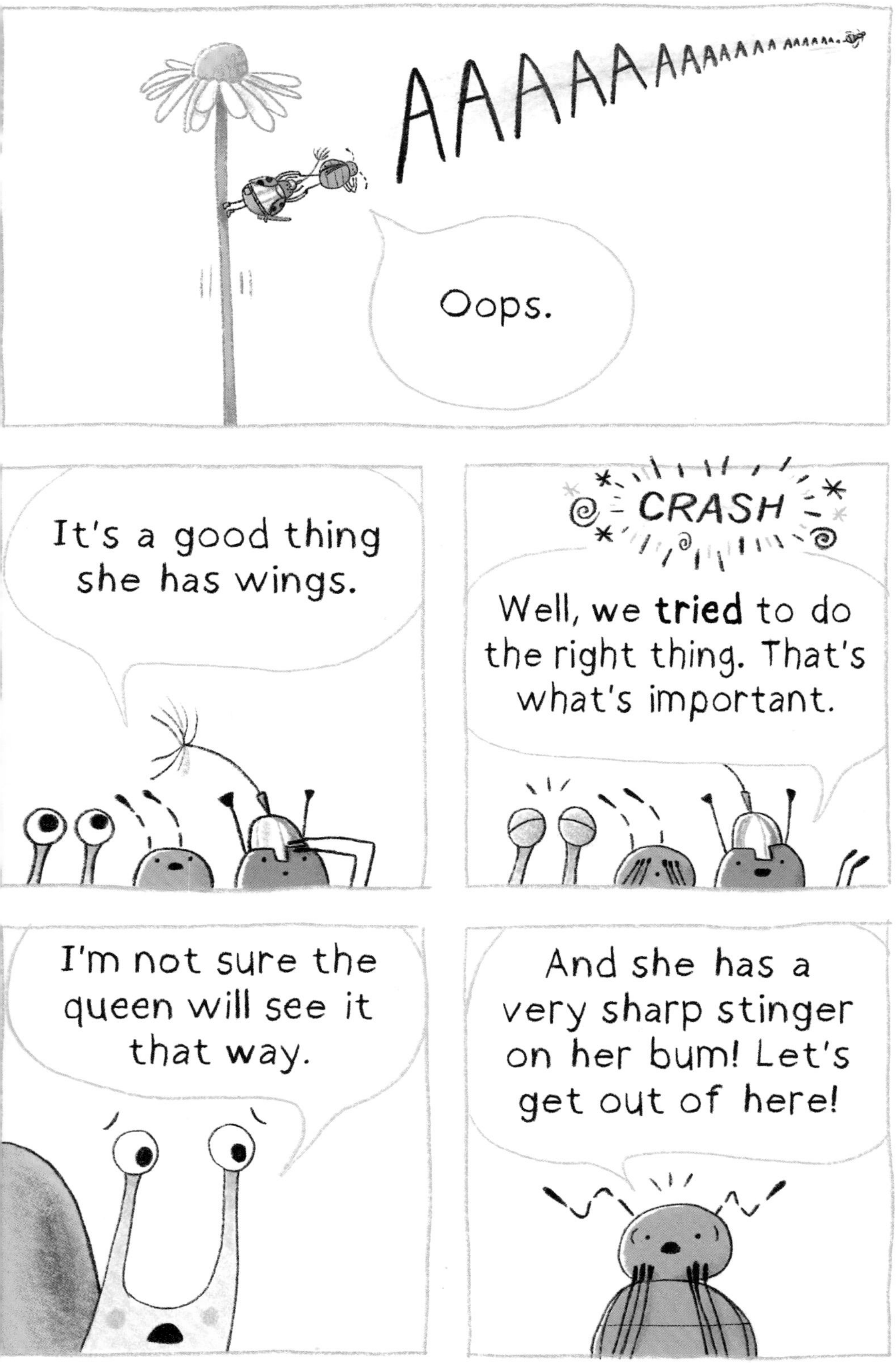
AAAAAAAAAAAAAAAAAA
Oops.
It's a good thing she has wings.
CRASH
Well, we **tried** to do the right thing. That's what's important.
I'm not sure the queen will see it that way.
And she has a very sharp stinger on her bum! Let's get out of here!

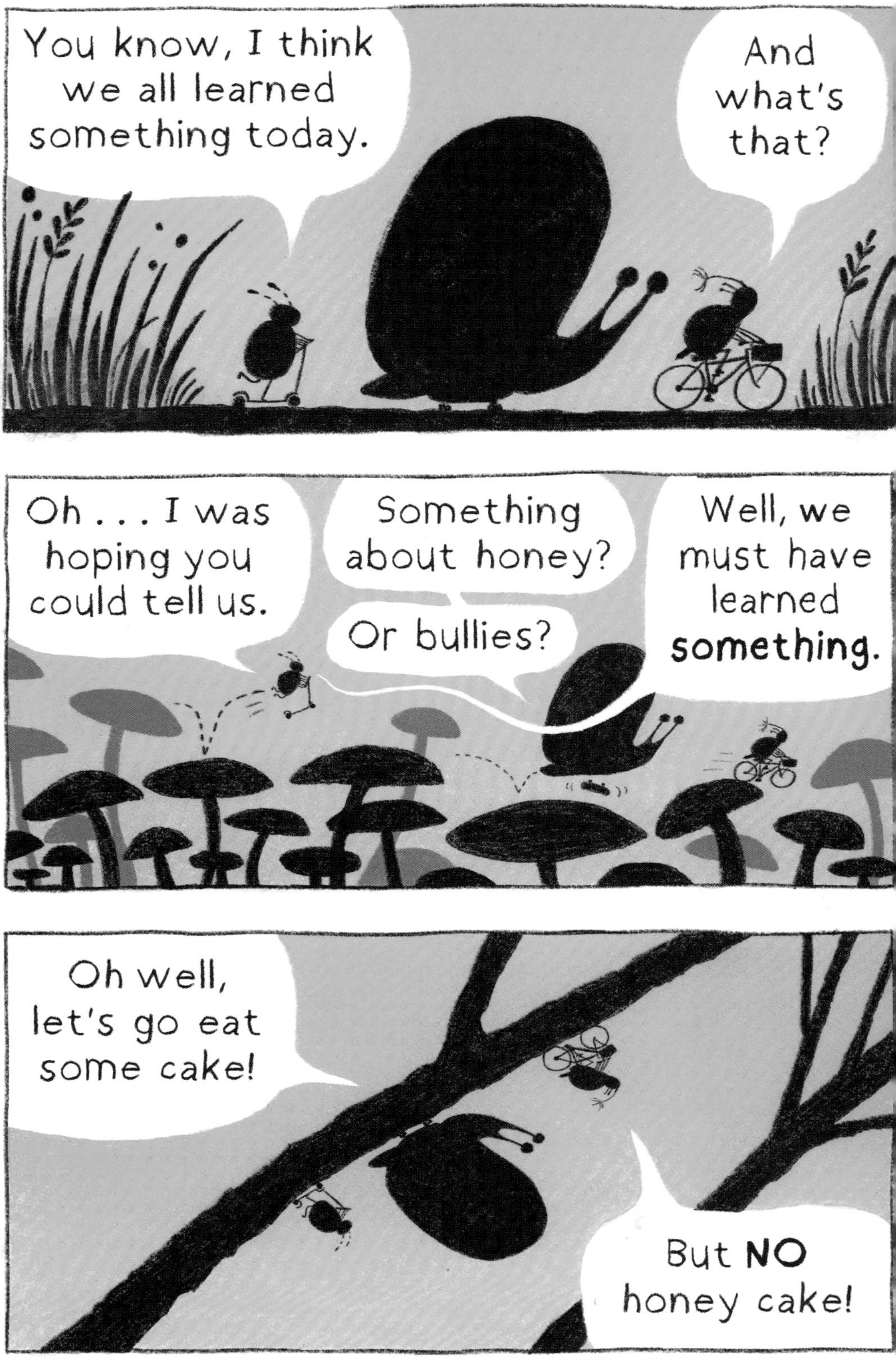
You know, I think we all learned something today.
And what's that?
Oh . . . I was hoping you could tell us.
Something about honey?
Or bullies?
Well, we must have learned **something**.
Oh well, let's go eat some cake!
But **NO** honey cake!

MORE ADVENTURES OF

SIR LADYBUG

SIR LADYBUG
Geisel Award Winner
Corey R. Tabor

SIR LADYBUG
and the
BOOKWORMS
Geisel Award Winner
Corey R. Tabor

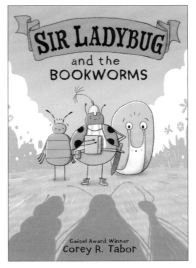

Just let me
get ready.

More from Corey R. Tabor

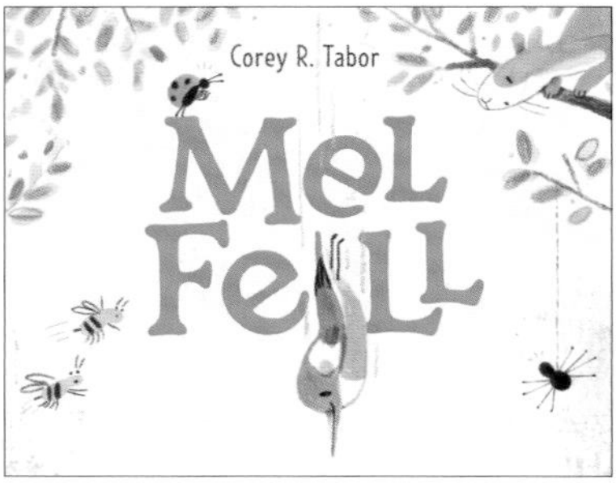
Corey R. Tabor
Mel Fell

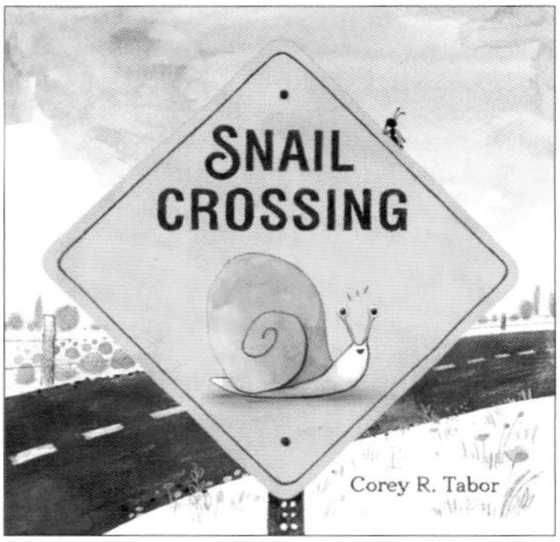
SNAIL CROSSING
Corey R. Tabor

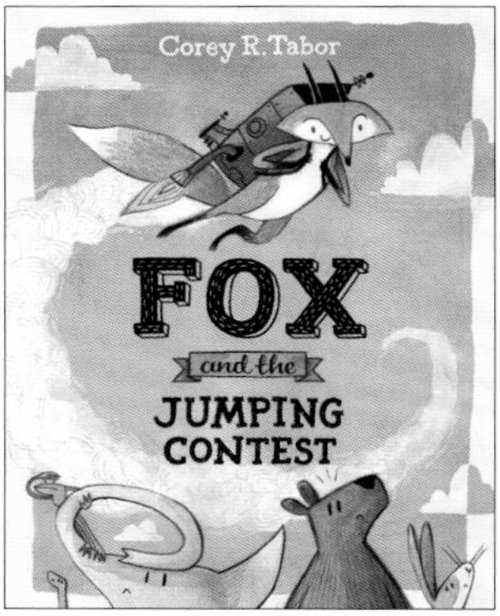
Corey R. Tabor
FOX and the JUMPING CONTEST

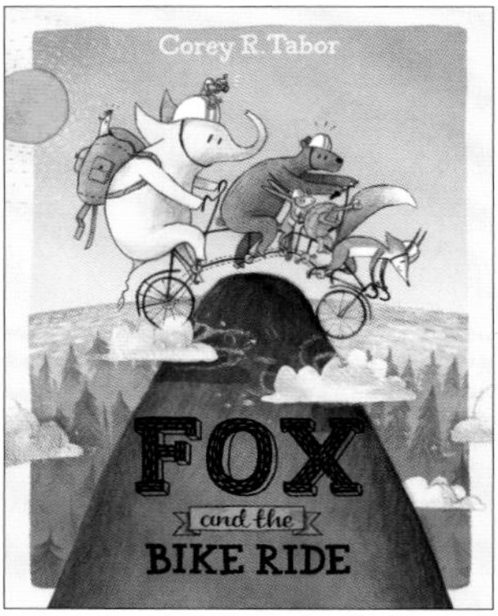
Corey R. Tabor
FOX and the BIKE RIDE

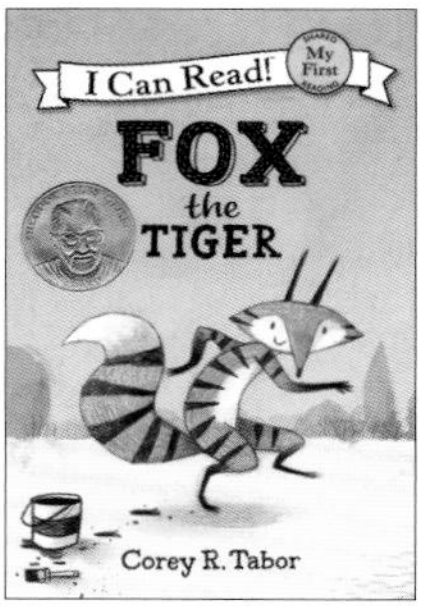
I Can Read!
My First
FOX the TIGER
Corey R. Tabor

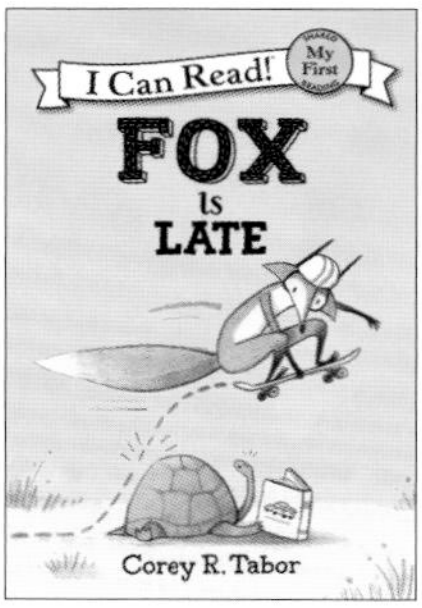
I Can Read!
My First
FOX is LATE
Corey R. Tabor

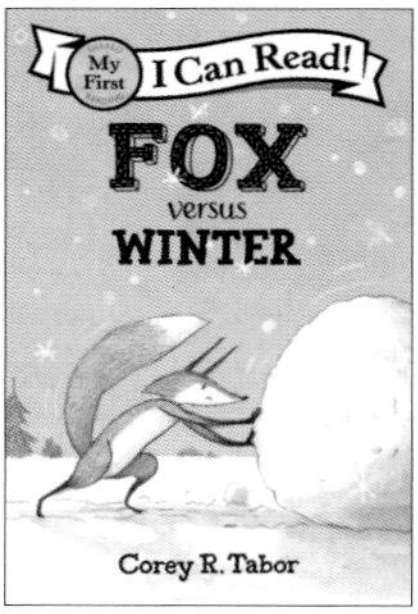
My First
I Can Read!
FOX versus WINTER
Corey R. Tabor

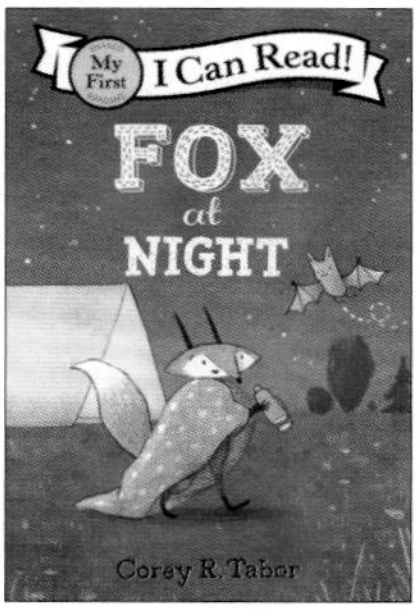
My First
I Can Read!
FOX at NIGHT
Corey R. Tabor

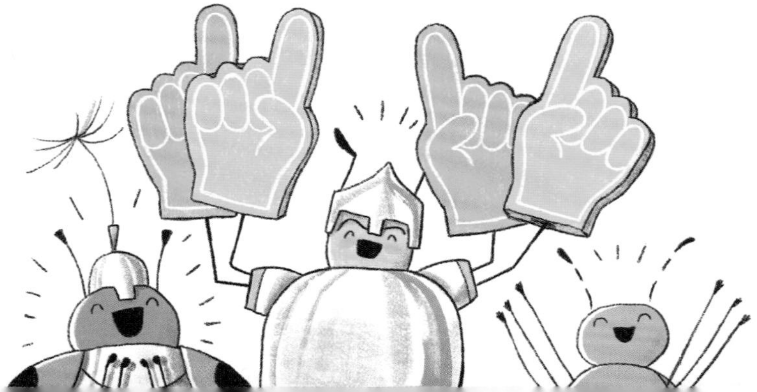